The Ghostwriter

of New Orleans

The Ghostwriter
of New Orleans

Laura Michaud

PELICAN PUBLISHING
New Orleans 2022

The word "Pelican" and the depiction of a pelican are trademarks of Arcadia Publishing Company Inc. and are registered in the U.S. Patent and Trademark Office.

ISBN 9781455626243
E-book ISBN 9781455626250

Printed in the United States of America

Published by Pelican Publishing
New Orleans, LA
www.pelicanpub.com

For Marc, Maddie, and Charlie.
Thank you for all the "writing time."
I love you.

And for Dr. Randy Clark.
Thank you for the amazing human being you were.
You are missed.

So we beat on, boats against the current,
borne back ceaselessly into the past.

F. Scott Fitzgerald,
The Great Gatsby

James

How many times have you forgotten to do something small? Shut a window before it rains? Grab your phone on your way out the door? Do up a button on your shirt? Pack your homework before you leave for school? On the day that seals my fate, I forget to look over my shoulder.

Nothing is unusual about the moments before it happens. I get the same rush of freedom that I always get when I leave the school parking lot, hit the gas, and turn onto St. Charles Avenue. The same line of live oak trees casts its tunnel of shadows over the street. I see their branches moving, so I turn the air-conditioning off, roll my windows down, ignore the text messages blowing up my phone, and turn the Jimi Hendrix music (that I only listen to when I am by myself) way up. The sweat starts to pool around the white collar of my school uniform, but the feeling of the wind across my face is totally worth it. I do not know that this is the last time I will ever experience it.

I guess if you asked me what I *do* know for sure in those last moments, I would say that I am a pretty fast runner, I am decent at guitar, and Margot Cramer is the love of my life.

When I forget to look over my shoulder, the streetcar hits my Toyota, and I swerve into a lamppost and then another car.

Music reverberates through my mind. It mixes with the high-pitched sound of a woman screaming. I want the music to drown her out, but it doesn't. Distant sirens spin around and around, getting louder with every repetition.

"Don't move him!" I hear a man's voice yell. He sounds far away, muffled.

"Move me!" I want to yell back. "Get me out!" I feel pressure coming from every side of me as if someone has stuffed me into a box that I am too big for.

"Hey!" another voice shouts. My eyes flutter open to see a panicked face that I do not recognize peering at me through fragmented lines of cracked glass.

The music is starting to slow. The once steady guitar notes are more like an intermittent drip from a leaky faucet. A weak drumbeat pulses within my body, but its timing feels off, and I try to will it to change. I feel a frustration that I don't have the energy for.

I hear the sound of groaning metal. There is a board underneath me. I'm moving. A tingling feeling takes over, though I can't pinpoint where it's coming from.

People are talking rapidly all around me, but I only pick up bits and pieces of what they're saying.

"Head."

"Pulse."

"Hurry."

I want the blue and red lights to stop flashing. I hear doors shut.

When I no longer hear the music or the sirens or any screaming, I close my eyes.

Margot

Margot Cramer slurps her iced coffee. The lady next to her looks up from her laptop and glares, but she ignores it. She needs to tell her boyfriend James that she will be leaving. It is not going to go well. She swallows. Of all the secrets she has been keeping, she is not sure why this one bothers her the most.

She picks up her phone again and glances at the time. He is fifteen minutes late. There is one new message, but not from him. She reads it with a heavy sigh. "I know," she types. "I'm waiting for James."

She cranes her head to look out the window. No sign of him. Condensation is starting to pool on the side of her plastic cup. It's always just a degree or so too warm in the coffee shop, and the ice waters down the drink faster than she can sip it. There isn't much she likes about the place—the owner's refusal to crank the air-conditioning, the cheap cups, the uncomfortable red plastic chairs—but it is close to home, and she loves the smell of coffee. And it is theirs.

Her fingers flick across the screen of her phone in rapid succession. When she is done, she rests it on the table and stares at the envelope sticking out of her backpack. The email came two days ago, but the letter arrived yesterday. The New York City return address sends a mini-wave of excitement through her that makes her stomach dip. Then it dips again, this time from nervousness when she thinks about showing it to James. She can just picture the way his eyebrows will probably rise up and then he'll exhale, a sigh big enough to lift the sand-colored hair that rests on his forehead into the air.

For a moment her eyes well up when she thinks about being without him every day. At first, school in New York and the internship that comes along with it seemed like such a great idea. And she'd be away from her mother. Now the reality of what it would mean to leave New Orleans is sinking in.

She had been caught up in the moment when her father first took her on the tour of the school. How would she explain to James that he wasn't an afterthought? That she had just been swept up in New York City, the newness of it all, and, if she was being honest, her dad's attention. The application seemed pointless at the time.

She picks at the muffin she bought. It's stale, but she chews on it and stares at the wall. He won't understand. She knows he won't. She'll see it in his eyes and it will break her heart. The same way it did when she told him she had to miss his district championship. The same way she felt when she saw him smile at Ez with that sparkle in his eyes normally reserved for her. This was worse, though. Longer lasting. It would mean no more weekend afternoons curled up on his couch, her head resting on his chest, binge-watching reality shows. No more peeking out her window to see if the light in his bedroom (across the street, two doors down, second floor all the way to the right) was on or off. No more of his quick hugs between classes. She thinks of the smell of him when he draws her in, the morning shower still fresh on him, his "before practice smell," she calls it.

She sniffles. They'll be okay. They have to be. Anna Malone went to boarding school, and she still hangs out with everyone when she comes home.

God, where is he already? He probably took forever getting out to the parking lot after school. Or forgot something again. She tips her chair back, folds her arms, and thinks for a little while about the English paper that she needs to work on tonight. There won't be time to do that and go to Kimberley's, so she is going to have to figure something out. Maybe get up early tomorrow morning.

She brings the chair back down to the ground harder

than she should, and this time she meets the perturbed look of the lady next to her with one of her own. She shifts her eyes toward the window again. The sun has ducked behind a cloud and it is darker now, but there is still no sign of him.

She picks up her phone again. "Really? Been waiting 30 minutes. Swing by your house later." She hesitates before sending it because she knows there probably won't be time for that too, but she really needs to talk to him and get this off her chest. For a moment she feels her throat tighten and her eyes begin to well again, this time out of frustration.

She can't keep Kimberley waiting much longer. She clears her throat, takes a sip of the watery coffee, and hits send. She picks up the latte she had ordered for him a half-hour ago to throw it away, but the brown plastic lid pops off, and she gasps until she realizes that the coffee that has spilled all over her lap is no longer hot.

The owner narrows his eyes at her from behind the counter but doesn't offer her a cloth or napkins. She thinks that maybe next time she'll complain. Maybe she'll tell him that it's too hot and the chairs are uncomfortable. But it doesn't matter. She'll never come back again.

James

When I open my eyes, I squint and struggle to get my bearings. I'm standing in the hallway of my high school, St. Xavier. It's early evening, and there's a soft, candlelit glow to the place. It has not yet been swept clean of the day's debris—wrappers, lost notebook pages, mud.

I suck in a breath and my eyes dart around as I struggle to remember why I came back. Did I forget something in my locker? Maybe my bio book? I am always forgetting that damn bio book.

I rub my eyes and walk in the direction of my locker. When I pass the gym, I hear the sound of shoes squeaking across the floor and a basketball hitting the backboard. Voices rebound back and forth.

What time is it? I pat my pockets for my phone. Has to be in my locker. That's probably why I've come back, I reason, weirded out by my inability to remember specifically.

I make the final turn to my locker and jog down the narrow hallway. This section must have been cleaned already because the lights are off and the stench of industrial cleaner hangs in the air.

14-27-14. I spin the dial of the lock and open the door.

The bio book is gone. I feel around on the top shelf for my phone, but it isn't there. Maybe my math book? Don't I have a math test coming up?

I am just about to grab the red geometry book when Mr. Fredericks, the history teacher, opens a classroom door and emerges into the dark hallway.

"Hey, Mr. Fredericks. Forgot my math book," I say, pointing to my locker.

His head is tilted, and he's balancing his phone between his ear and his shoulder as he struggles with a bag.

"Yes, I'm just leaving now," he says into the phone as he turns his back to me and starts down the hallway.

I shrug and mutter, "Me too . . ." as I grab my book, slam my locker, and head in the opposite direction to the student parking lot.

I lean into the heavy double door, punching the metal bar with my elbow and emerging onto the top step overlooking the lot. It is empty, except for a red Jeep. No sign of my blue Toyota. I exhale. Anxiety begins to rise from the pit of my stomach.

Maybe I parked out front? Risked the parking ticket because I thought I'd be in and out? I clench my jaw and run my hands through my hair.

I burst back through the door and run toward the front entrance. I pass a tall guy leaning against a locker with his arms folded. His eyes follow me as I make my way along the length of the hallway. I don't recognize him, but I slow my pace and ask, "Hey, do you know what time it is?"

He comes closer and extends his hand. "I'm Stewart."

I pause. I'm struggling to make sense of his appearance. He's tall, with a head of black curly hair and a wide smile. I search his face for something familiar, but his eyes give nothing away and just return a bright, steady gaze.

"You're confused," he says. "It's okay. I can help."

He's not wrong. I am confused. I have the same hazy feeling you get when you open your eyes for the first time in the morning. I keep blinking, trying to reset my focus.

Stewart's clothes are different. It's a St. Xavier's uniform but not the same one that I have four identical versions of at home. He notices me staring at it and then says, "I would have been the class of 1990. It's a little dated." He smiles.

"Why are you wearing it then?" I manage after another awkward moment of silence. I swallow hard.

"Oh," Stewart furrows his brow. "Well, this was the uniform the year that I died."

I step backward, looking for someone who might be able to help. "Look, I don't know where you came from, but you're not supposed to be in here." I stammer, "I . . . I just came to get a book. I'm leaving . . ."

"But James, you can't." There is an eerie expression of pity on his face.

"How do you know my name?" I ask, backing up again.

"I'm sorry, it's not always obvious at first. Sometimes people arrive without the memory of having passed. I could let you wander around figuring everything out for a while, but I thought I would spare you that."

"What are you talking about?" I hate how scared my voice sounds, and I pad around my pockets, looking for my cell phone. Maybe I can get in a fast dial to 911 before this dude makes a move.

"Look, you should know first of all that everything is going to be alright," Stewart continues. He extends his palms in the air like he is surrendering. "You are not alone. There are others besides us."

I bolt. I run towards the main entrance where the door opens to a busy street and there should be people around to help me.

"There's no need to be scared!" I hear him yelling after me, but I continue to sprint and then burst through the front doors and down the sprawling front steps.

Cars zoom by in the dense rush hour traffic. When I reach the bottom of the stairs, I spot a woman wearing earphones jogging by. I wave my arms and shout to get her attention, but her straightforward gaze doesn't change.

I let out a groan, half exasperation, half panic, and sprint again toward the sidewalk, trying to flag down a passing car instead. But the second I take my first step onto the cement, I bounce backward and find myself back on the lawn. I spring up and attempt to run once more, only to find myself laid out on the grass again.

Panic pulses through me now. None of this can be happening. When am I just going to wake up? I glance up at the entrance to the school.

Stewart stands at the top of the stairs waving.

"Nobody is going to hurt you, James," he calls. "Everything is okay. Please let me explain to you what's going on."

A phone. I need a phone. I scramble to stand and take off running towards the back entrance of the school. I find it propped open by two rolling garbage cans and a mop that sits outside of it.

I pump my arms harder and harder with each step and begin to yell, "Mr. Franklin! Mr. Franklin! I need help!" But when I reach the entrance there's no sign of the janitor anywhere. I pause, listening for his characteristic whistling while he cleans. Nothing.

"Mr. Franklin!" I yell again. No response, so I take off in the direction of the main office.

It's dark, with the small blinds down, covering the door's glass window. Even though I expect it to be locked, I still rattle the doorknob with a sense of desperation.

"Damn it!" I glance over both shoulders. Nobody is coming. I take a deep breath and gear up to punch the glass. I look away from the door, not wanting to see my own blood when my fist breaks through the window. But when I make contact with the glass there is no sound of it shattering. Confused, I reach through to feel for the lock. It's a simple click, and I'm in.

In front of me is Sister Ellen's desk. She's long gone, but her yellow wool cardigan hangs over the back of the chair, and I send it flying across the room as I trip to get to the phone.

"Dial nine first," I remind myself, trying to steady my hand and hearing in my head Sister Ellen's monotone response to every child who has ever asked to call home.

9-9-1-1. It rings three times.

"New Orleans 911, what is your emergency?"

"Yes, I'm a student at St. Xavier High School." I gulp back tears of relief at the sound of help.

"Hello?"

"Yes, I'm a student at St. Xavier High School," I repeat. "Something's wrong. I'm stuck at the school and there's some guy in here following me!"

"Hellooooo?"

"Hello, can you hear me?"

"I got a call from St. Xavier's school coming in, but ain't nobody on the line," I hear the now muffled voice say. "Hello, this is New Orleans 911. Is someone there?"

"Yes!" I plead. "Yes, can you hear me?" No response and then a dial tone. I put the phone back on the receiver and resist the urge to fall to pieces.

"Just a bad connection," I reason, steadying myself on the desk with both hands. "Just try again." But before I can, I am startled by the loud and frantic double ring of an incoming call on the office phone. A square button is flashing red. I press it and pick the receiver back up.

"Hello? This is New Orleans 911. Is someone there?"

"Yes, please help me," I choke out. "I'm a student, and . . ."

"It picked up but still ain't nobody on the other line. I got someone on the way to check it out. Hello? If someone is there and you can hear me, police are on the way."

I drop the receiver down on the desk and stare at it. Minutes pass. I wait and wait, every creak of the building causing me to startle and turn.

"Hi." I look up to see a small blonde girl in the doorway. She glances over her shoulder and then back at me.

"You better get in here," I say, fatigue starting to set into my voice. "I don't know what's going on, but there's this weird guy, and I can't get out. I think the police are coming."

"Okay," she says, taking a step inside the office. "I'll wait here with you then." I note her lack of urgency but watch as she sits down in the desk chair.

"You saw him too?" I ask. "He's pretty tall. Has some weird old uniform on?"

She nods, not taking her blue eyes off me but looking undisturbed.

"Did he talk to you? He was saying all sorts of crazy stuff about dying and . . ."

I suddenly hear a radio barking orders and footsteps coming down the hallway.

"I been here all afternoon," I hear Mr. Franklin's voice say. "And I ain't seen nothing."

"Office door usually open this time of day?" responds another voice as the radio continues to pop. A flashlight dances around at different angles.

"It wasn't like that before when I cleaned up this corridor!" Mr. Franklin exclaims.

"Call came from the main office, it seems. This one the main office?"

"Yes, sir, it is."

I rush out from behind the desk as the voices grow closer.

"In here! I'm the one who called!" I say as they enter and flick on the lights.

"Looks like someone's definitely been in here," the cop continues, and they both walk right past me into the office.

My mouth hangs open, and I look behind me at the girl in the chair. She meets my eyes and shakes her head.

"They can't see me either," she says. "I'm sorry."

Margot

She replays it in her head now, in the pitch blackness of her bedroom. Her mother tracking her down and then picking her up from Kimberley's in the silver Volvo station wagon. The eerie blank expression on her face as she ushered her to the car and whisked her away in silence. Calmly telling her to turn off her phone and put it away until they get home. The whole time Margot thinking she was just in trouble for not being where she was supposed to be. Apologizing the second they walked in the kitchen door because she couldn't stand the silence anymore.

"Look, Mom, I'm sorry. I know I said I'd be at the coffee shop, but James was late and Kimberley needed some help with her English paper, so—"

"Margot, sit down, honey." Her mother leaning onto the kitchen counter hard with one arm.

Noticing how pale her mother's face was, her heart quickening.

"Mom, what's wrong?"

Her mother's lips pursing as she rubbed at her temple. "Something tragic has happened."

Margot leaning hard into the wooden back of the kitchen chair. "What? What is going on?"

Her mother walking over to her and kneeling down in front of her. Taking Margot's hands in hers. "I'm so sorry to have to tell you this," her voice cracking as she swallowed hard. "But James was killed in a car accident after school."

Margot had felt the grip tighten around her hands, but all around the rest of her, nothingness. Her chin dropped, and when she could, she focused her stare back on her mother.

"What?" she asked, looking at her mother's face for a hint of anything that would signal that what she had just said was not true, even though Margot knew this was something you never lie about, was just trying to buy a few more moments before it had to be real. Her mother closed her eyes and nodded.

It was hard to know if she screamed inside her head or out loud. She had felt her body shaking, felt her mother's arms around her.

Then she couldn't breathe. She was coughing and choking and her mother began rushing back and forth for napkins, a glass of water, anything that would help.

"What happened?" she said when she could steady her breath.

"It happened on St. Charles," her mother began, pulling another chair across from her and sitting down. "We don't really know the details. It was a collision. His injuries were too great . . ."

Margot began shaking her head, trying to clear her mind's eye before it started to form any visuals for her.

"He never met me after school," she said. Her mother nodded at her.

She began to feel cold, to rock back and forth.

"How did you find out?" She wasn't sure why she asked this, why it even mattered.

"Mr. Therioult called me." Margot closed her eyes and pictured his parents. His mother's big smile, his dad's sideways hugs.

"I'm freezing," she said.

"You're in shock. Let's get you a blanket." Her mother had walked her up to her bedroom with one arm around her the whole way. They lay on her bed together, Margot swaddled in a quilt, her mother behind her squeezing harder with every sob.

"I'm so sorry, baby," she whispered. "I'm so sorry."

She must have faded out at some point, but now she opens her eyes to stare across the room at her mother, who is sitting upright in an armchair, asleep. The only thing illuminating the room is her mother's cellphone that suddenly sputters alive on her lap and then goes faint again. Margot thinks about her own phone for a moment and then, realizing she has nothing to say to anyone, realizing she cannot stand to tap into the questions that begin to roll around her mind, ask for details that she isn't ready to explore—she shuts her eyes tight.

She doesn't leave her room at all the next day. Instead, she lays her in bed, still in her school uniform, which uncomfortably bunches up every time she shifts, blinking at the branches of the massive tree outside her window. Squirrels and birds carry on as if it's just a regular day. As if the whole world has not shifted. She digs a fingernail into her forearm to make sure that she is awake and that this is real.

When her mother comes in to check on her, she pretends she is asleep. It feels easier than answering any questions. Easier than hearing any more details. They don't matter anyway. He's gone. The shock has subsided and now she can feel the weight of his absence sitting on her chest. She thinks about asking for her phone. Thinks about picking little pieces of him off of it—his words or pictures of him— to soothe herself but it also feels too painful. It's easier to stare out the window and let everything outside do all the work of carrying on instead.

She hears her mother whispering loudly on the phone outside of her room.

"I need to go sit with Patricia and Charles, but there is no way I can leave Margot. You know, I called Bob to tell him. You'd think he might fly down here to be with his daughter, but no. He's leaving for Los Angeles tomorrow, so just keep him posted. I know, I know. What did I really expect?"

She wakes again to a knock on her door. She doesn't answer but hears the sound of it opening, followed by Kimberley's voice.

"Margot?"

She stares at the wall. Feels Kimberley sit down on the end of her bed.

"Margot?" she says again, her voice cracking a little. Margot takes a deep breath and exhales silently. She does not want to listen to Kimberley cry.

"Hey," she says, rolling over and then looking at the ceiling.

"I've been trying to call you. Your mom said she wasn't sure if you turned your phone back on, so I thought I'd just come."

"I didn't," she replies. "I just can't yet."

"I get it," Kimberley whispers.

Margot begins to feel sick to her stomach so she sits up and hugs her knees. She meets eyes with her friend and they both tear up. Kimberley reaches out to hug her and Margot clings to her.

"I'm so sorry, I don't even know what to say," Kimberley says through sobs.

"I can't believe he's gone, Kim. How can he be gone?" Margot cries into her shoulder.

"I know. Nobody can believe it. It just doesn't seem real." Margot's cheek presses into her friend's soft, long brown hair, and she hugs her tighter.

They are silent for a minute and then Margot pulls away.

"I think they're trying to organize something for him at school," Kimberley says, straightening up and sniffling.

Margot shakes her head. "I'm not going."

"So everyone can come together and remember him."

"I'm not going," she repeats, laying back down. "I don't want to go back there. Ever." But then she thinks, how could she not? How could she not go back and try to pick up every piece of what's left of him there? Her eyes well up again.

Kimberley nods and watches her friend stare out the window.

The damn birds are chirping again, and Margot hears the mail truck rattle by. She closes her eyes and pulls the blankets over her head. She wishes Kimberley would go so that she can get the pills out of her closet.

James

The blonde girl rises from the office chair and takes a few steps towards me. She's small and unthreatening, and I don't flinch as she puts a hand on my arm.

"I'm so sorry. There's always an adjustment period, but when you don't remember your death, it makes it so much harder. I went through something similar. It was terrifying." Mr. Franklin and the cop are carrying on, flicking on lights throughout the various offices. "Come on, let's at least move out into the hallway."

I feel the urge to cry. I can't really be dead. But then, why can't people see me? I put my face in my hands as we walk. When the hell am I going to wake up?

She continues to pat my arm and says, "I know it feels like a dream, as if it can't be real."

I feel exhausted. I sink to the ground and stare at my shoes. How could these same shoes have walked an alive me through these very same hallways? How am I here but not here? She sits next to me in silence, twisting a strand of hair around her index finger, waiting.

"So, what am I supposed to do?" I ask in a flat voice without looking at her.

"Right now just try to relax. Things will stabilize. I mean, you won't always feel this emotional." Her voice is soft and calm, but I can't shake the confusion or the anger I feel. "The most important thing to remember is that you're here for a reason."

"I died, and I'm in my high school. For a *reason?*"

"I know. I know how it sounds. But yes, that's the case."

"So the guy I saw before? He's dead too?"

"Stewart? Yes. I'm sorry he scared you. He's been here for so long, I think he's forgotten what a shock the initial crossing over can be."

"How did I die?"

"I don't know. We probably won't know that until school opens tomorrow. You might not have noticed this yet, but we're not able to leave the school grounds."

I think of the early morning chaos in the hallways. It's hard to picture talk of my death mixed in with the normal sounds of lockers slamming and students yelling. I picture Margot waiting by my locker and put my head in my hands.

"Crap, Margot . . ."

"You're thinking of a friend?"

I nod and close my eyes. I remember leaving school for the coffee shop. I think of Margot waiting for me there. How she never knew that I would purposefully come in the side entrance because the extra steps meant she couldn't see me coming, and I love the look on her face when she suddenly sees me. That look would only last a couple of seconds before she'd point out the parking spots right out front. I wonder how long she waited for me today, and sadness comes at me like a strong, cold breeze.

Then my thoughts turn to my mother and father. What's going on in my house at this very moment? I picture my mother on the tan sofa sobbing, and I swallow hard.

"Was it just me?" I ask.

"Hmm?"

"Did I die alone?"

She exhales. "I wish I could tell you. Again, you won't have a lot of those answers until school opens tomorrow."

"Why?"

"Well, like I said, you'll hear the faculty and students discussing it, and—"

"No. WHY?" I interrupt. "Why this? Why am I . . . here?" I motion all around me at the deserted locker bays and the linoleum floors.

"Oh. Well, it's complicated, James, but the short answer is to protect them. The students."

I shake my head. Cobwebs are starting to fill it again. Maybe if I just let them take over, I'll sleep a deeper sleep, escape from this . . . whatever it is.

She leans her head to the side to meet my far-off gaze.

"It's a lot to absorb. There's more, but why don't we get you to a place where you can rest for a while. The thing is, your emotions, your attachments to their world will start to dull every day you're here. It has to, really, for you to be able to be here and do what's needed of you. You'll see. Come on." She stands and motions to me to join her.

She is barely making sense to me but what options do I have? I look up at her hovering above me, and I stand.

I jolt awake and sit straight up. I blink repeatedly to focus and realize that I am sitting on the bleachers by the football field.

"You're safe," I hear a voice say. I turn to see the blonde girl, sitting with her back propped up at the other end of the bleachers. "You probably feel calmer, anyway."

She's right. I'm aware of everything going on around me—the sounds of passing cars, the sun creeping halfway over the field—but I also don't have that same feeling of dread tightening in my chest. I wonder why she is still with me.

"I love being able to sleep outside," she says, rising and stepping down a few rows to where I sit. I scoot back a little and watch her. "Especially when you can't feel the mosquitos or the heat. We spend a lot of time outside. It's kind of our peace from them." She motions towards the school building with her head, then smoothes her gray uniform skirt and sits down next to me. I open my mouth to speak, but she beats me to it.

"My name is Gabriella. Do you remember us meeting yesterday?"

I nod, remembering her strange behavior in the office, the way that she had looked at me with such understanding in her eyes, the calm tone of her voice in response to my panicked one.

"So, how are you feeling?" she asks.

"Okay, just a little . . ."

"Foggy? It's normal. You're transitioning. You're starting to numb to some of the emotions you needed to get by when you were alive."

I nod, not because I understand but because I want her to stop talking. I take her in again. Her frizzy blonde hair comes down to her shoulders, and her uniform seems too big for her tiny frame, like someone dressed up a doll in the wrong clothes. She meets my eyes and I look away. We are silent.

"I don't know what I am supposed to do," I finally say. The thought comes out of my mouth before I intend to speak it. Despite the calmness I can't shake the cloud of confusion that surrounds me or the need to make sense of things.

"That's okay," she says, bringing her knees to her chest and looking out at the field. "We will help you. Stewart—you met him already—he'll help you with all the rules around here. Besides us there is Ali." I don't respond, but she keeps talking. "Stewart is the guy that scared you. He didn't mean to scare you though, I promise. He's just been here so long that he forgets that being a ghost isn't exactly the norm."

Ghost. I let the word rattle around in my brain for a minute and try to find a place to take root, and then I turn my eyes away from her and towards the track. I freeze at the sight of a coach and a student, their backs to the bleachers, deep in conversation.

Who is that? I don't recognize the silhouette of either of them. I narrow my eyes and notice that they are lighter than their surroundings, as if someone has painted them in water colors.

The coach paces up and down a small section of the green grass as the student stretches from side to side.

"They're residuals. Just leftover energy of people who have been here through the years that the school has been in existence," Gabriella says in an even-keeled voice as the boy begins to jog in place. "They're not really here. Not in the way that you and I are. Or the students and teachers are."

I close my eyes and shake my head, and when I open them they are still there. The boy is running at full speed around the track now, and the coach's mouth is open as if screaming at him, but there is no sound coming out.

"They come in bursts and then disappear," she adds.

The boy fades first. I stare at the odd vision of the coach, his face gnarled, his mouth open in a large "O," screaming at nothing. He grows lighter and lighter, and then he is gone too. I put my head in my hands.

"I know," Gabriella says with a small laugh that makes me cringe. "It's a lot. It's a lot to take in. You'll see them around from time to time though, so don't be scared. They're harmless, but they're important. They're actually how we know things are functioning alright around here."

"But really . . . why am I here?" I ask, looking away from the faded figures. I stand and cross my arms, looking out at the track that had been such a big part of my daily alive life.

I realize it at that moment: my stutter is gone. The words have been coming out unbroken. I remember my mother's voice during speech therapy when I was little saying, "That was a smooth one," as she would smile and stroke my hair. I close my eyes again, hoping that will help me avoid thinking about home right now.

Gabriella's voice interrupts my efforts. "You're a protector."

"What?" I say, turning in her direction.

"That's why you're here." She pauses for a moment and then continues, "When you die young, sometimes you need to help protect others before you can move on. That's about as simple as I can make it for you, James."

"Who? Who am I protecting?"

"Who?" She stretches her arms above her head and moves her neck from side to side. "Nobody really knows, James. Maybe you're here for someone in particular. Maybe you're here for a bunch of them. You just keep at it every day and whenever it happens, whenever you've achieved what you are here for, you'll move on. Stewart will explain it more when you have your orientation."

"Margot," I whisper.

"Could be," she shrugs. "There were people from my year that I was sure I was here to protect too. Turns out that wasn't the case."

"How long have you been here?"

"Nine years," she says and looks over at the field.

"Nine years?"

"Yes, nine years. Just because you have good work to do doesn't mean it will go quickly!" I watch from the corner of my eye as she begins to bite at her nails. "Sorry," she says standing up. "I didn't mean to snap at you."

"So, what now?"

"Well, I thought it might be better for you to be outside this morning. It'll be heavy in there. You died yesterday, and they'll all be talking about it, grieving. It might be tough, even with some numbing." She shrugs. "Stewart's in there trying to get you some answers."

Car doors are slamming and the student lot is starting to fill up.

"Like I said, it's probably for the best."

I sigh. All around me the school is starting to transform with the sounds of voices, car stereos, the tinny screech of school bus brakes.

"I'm going to go in."

She raises her eyebrows. "Okay." She nods. "I'll come with you."

We make our way down the bleachers and to the double doors that lead into the gym. My footsteps across the grass feel airy, my body feels as if I'm floating in a pool.

I spot Stewart coming outside from one of the gym doors. He's coming towards us, hands in his pockets.

"He's doing okay," Gabriella says when he reaches us.

Stewart smiles and looks at the ground before speaking. "Hey, James. I'm Stewart. I'm sorry that I scared you yesterday. I was just trying to help."

"It's fine," I say, looking past him.

"It was a car accident." Stewart says it first to Gabriella and then meets my eyes. "Something about a collision with a streetcar."

"I hit a streetcar?" My mouth hangs open.

"Or it hit you. I didn't get too many details. It will all start to come back to you after a while." He glances behind him at the doors. "The grief counselors are setting up some stations in the gym right now. We can go in if you want to, look around a little before your orientation."

I enter through the doors without opening them. I might have taken a moment to be amazed at what I'd just done if it wasn't for the sights in front of me. Four white pop-up tents are set up in the corners of the gym. Chairs squeak across the floor as adults scurry to arrange them in groups.

Mrs. Burns, the school counselor, stands in the middle of it all with a clipboard, her head darting back and forth, surveying the scene. She has on black dress pants that look strained around her belly, a wrinkled green blouse tucked into them, and a blue ribbon pinned to her chest.

"Okay!" she attempts to shout, but it comes out garbled. She clears her throat and tries again. "Okay! Hello everyone! If I could just have your attention for a moment, please." Chatter begins to trail off and the room falls silent.

"Good morning and thank you for coming. We of course had to put this together on very short notice, so I am extremely grateful to you all for being here. We expect this loss will hit the student community very hard, and I think this makeshift counseling center will be quite important in supporting the children these first few days." She clears her throat again and fumbles for her glasses that hang from a chain around her neck.

"Upon arriving at school, the students have been directed to the auditorium, where Principal Logan will share with them the difficult news. Of course, so many of them already know, and they have come to school today to connect with each other, to grieve together. I will be heading to the assembly as well to let them know that we have this resource here for them." She gestures around the room with an arm. "Now, to reiterate what many of you have already been told about James. He was a student-athlete, a quiet boy but well-liked. He was fatally injured last night in a collision."

I look around at the attentive faces that soften as she begins to speak about me.

"We've identified a few children that I will meet with individually. But as you know, this school was rattled last year by the drug overdose death of another student. Many of these children are still dealing with the trauma of her loss as well."

She's talking about Ali Townsend. We had not been friends, but everyone heard the gossip: that her boyfriend had gotten her the heroin after she begged and begged him to but then left her at the party when some older guy she'd been rumored to be hooking up with showed up. That guy dropped her home, and she died in her bed. Parents found her the next morning. There's another version that she was alive the next morning and died in an ambulance on the way to the hospital. Depended on who was telling it.

Is that what will happen with me, I wonder. Will there be different versions of how I died when I didn't even have my own version to hang on to yet?

Gabriella and Stewart emerge on each side of me. Or maybe they were there for some time, and I hadn't noticed. Gabriella puts her hand on my shoulder.

"The important thing to remember," Stewart says in a low voice, "is that everyone is where they are supposed to be. You are supposed to be here, and they are supposed to be alive."

I shake my head in annoyance. It's true that I'm not feeling the same agitation that I had last night, but I was getting tired of all the advice they keep doling out as I struggle to make sense of things on my own. Gabriella removes her hand.

Mrs. Burns continues to speak. "Now, we'll have this open throughout the day for children who find they want to come either on their own or as a group. James was a member of the track team, and I'll be checking in with Coach Samuels to see if he wants me to have a group meeting with them. Otherwise, we will just respond to the needs as they arise." Accommodating nods fill the room as she peeks at her watch. "Oh, and one more thing before I leave for the auditorium. Principal Logan felt that some sort of ribbon system," she pauses and points to the blue ribbon on her blouse, "would be a nice way to unify the school as we remember James. My understanding is that the parents' association is working hard to assemble these. Boxes of them should be delivered later today."

I let out a laugh of disbelief. I have my own ribbon? Gabriella and Stewart look at me with that same mixture of concern and pity that I'm already tired of, and something about the way they keep telling me what I am supposed to do is starting to piss me off.

Margot

She doesn't go to the memorial service. It's not stubbornness or grief, she just knows that she physically can't. At first, her mother is gentle but insistent. She tries the angle of how comforting it will be for the Therioults to have her there, but eventually, this backfires. What comfort could she possibly be? If she isn't crying, her mind goes to an eerily quiet place, where she sees James laying on his bed with his earphones on, stretched-out Nike socks hanging off his feet. Or hovered over a bowl of cereal at the kitchen counter, watching ESPN. She doesn't know how she will ever be able to pass their yellow house with the white fence ever again. Twice she has woken up from a dream where they were joking around and he gave her a playful shove, his brown eyes dancing the way they did when he forgot himself and really laughed.

Later her mother says something about closure. She might have used the word regret too, Margot doesn't know. She had been tuning her out and tracing the squares on her quilt at the time. She stood firm on not attending the service but had allowed herself to be talked into a lavender bubble bath and clean pajamas.

Every once in a while, she can hear her mother's work friend Evelyn, commissioned to be there so that Margot wouldn't be alone, coughing downstairs and talking to the cat. She looks at the clock on her white nightstand and realizes she hasn't seen her phone in three days, but she doesn't care. 11:10 am. The pill she took has kicked in, and his service has started.

Sometimes strange moments of practicality flood her

mind and force her to think about things going forward with a weird lucidity that scares her because it also feels like a betrayal. She pictures new routines at school. Who will she talk to now between periods? Alternatives for after school hangout spots. She knows this time in her room will run out, that eventually she won't be allowed to hide like this. The thought makes her chest tighten. How will she ever go back? How can things ever be normal again?

She thinks about New York and how she never got to tell him about it. She looks up at the ceiling and says out loud, "I got into Everton Fine Arts."

"Margot? You need something, honey?" Evelyn calls from the bottom of the stairs.

"No, I'm good," she says. But this, of course, is a lie. She hasn't been well for a while. And now it feels like everything can only get worse.

James

I didn't go to the assembly. I couldn't stand the thought of watching people talk about my life.

Instead, I fall into my own routine. For the next couple of days, I adopt the top row of the bleachers by the field and stay there, stretching out with my arms propped up underneath my head, staring up and fluctuating between disbelief and sleep, the sky a whole new mystery to stare at. Whenever my thoughts wander to my loved ones and my emotions seem like they might choke me, I fade out, as if someone has just given me a shot of a tranquilizer. It's like having the flu. I'd open my eyes to find Gabriella, smiling at me like she might offer me some soup and crackers, and then as she reassures me, her face goes fuzzy again.

My first night on the bleachers it pours a familiar type of New Orleans rainstorm, pounding massive drops that almost seem to blast bullet holes through me, and the realization that I wasn't getting wet, that the rain wasn't really bothering me, just made my energy level and lack of will to move even worse.

The next morning I wake up to find the track team, fully dressed in their red and white meet uniforms, spread out around the track, each on one knee, heads bowed. I sit up and squint. They looked unreal in the fragments of morning light, like statues surrounding the dewy grass. I didn't trust my eyes so I forced myself to take tired steps to the bottom of the stands until I reached the clay track and stared. After a few minutes Coach Samuels blew the whistle and called, "Bring it in." They jogged to him in the middle, each put a hand in, raised it, and shouted, "James!" Then they circled the track, sticking together like a swarm of bees, long faces, eyes toward the ground, and I felt the vibrations of their feet, the small gust of a breeze they created as they passed me. I watched their serious faces and wondered what each of them was thinking. Bradley, Peter, and Kyle, my best running buddies, occasionally sniffled and wiped at their faces. I sat on the ground and continued to stare at them. Feelings of sadness poked at me like stingers that never broke the skin.

Sometimes when I wake up from the numbing, I can remember that my mind has wandered to another place, captured details of my life for me, and they hang in the back of my memory like cobwebs. I can remember weird things like how cold the tiles of our kitchen floor could be on bare feet, or the roughness of the knitted throw blanket on the couch in the den, or the rotten smell of my ten-year-old black lab Bear's breath when he licks your face.

Other times when I am not sleeping I picture my mother in my room, crying on my bed. And I have a reoccurring vision of my father staring out the living room window. I'm unsure if this is just what I imagine them doing or if I have some strange ability to see glimmers of them somehow since it seems so realistic.

But the ones that wake me up out of this deep sleep, or coma-like trance, or whatever the hell it is, are of Margot. Sometimes I sit up straight on the steel bleacher, the night quiet but for the occasional blast of cicadas, and I can see her. Not right in front of me or anything like that. But like a silent movie in my mind's eye. Margot reaching over and zipping my backpack up completely—she hated it when there was even a two-inch gap before where the zipper ended. Margot talking with her hands to me in her kitchen while eating ice cream directly out of the carton with a spoon. Margot sitting by herself at the picnic table outside, waiting for me after school, jotting thoughts down in her notebook—the one with the cover that closed by winding a string around a large button.

When this happens my shoulders tense up for a few minutes and sadness feels like it's a batch of hives breaking out all over me until I can't stand another minute of it. Then it passes slowly, and I'm left with just the memory that a memory happened. It's not painful, just feels like a sore muscle that needs to be worked out.

I am not sure how many days it has been when I decide that I have enough energy to get up again. I am tired of being still, and I need to figure out what's happening to me. But even before that, I want to look for Margot. So I get up and make my way into the school.

Around me, things carry on like a normal day. The volume in the hallway is loud and people move around me at their usual fast pace.

"I never even saw that kid before," I hear one boy say to another as one of the PTA moms wanders the hall passing out the navy blue ribbons. I scan the corridor for Margot. I can see one of the "residuals," as Gabriella called them. It walks up to the water fountain next to the boys and turns the water on to get a drink. The boys look down at the running water with annoyance, just another glitch of an old building.

"Yeah. I don't know. He was a runner or something," the other boy finally responds.

I fold my arms and lean back against the locker bay. The not knowing is fair, I guess. Those who did know me really only knew me because I had been around since elementary school. But even then, I didn't speak much in grade school because of the stutter.

By the time the schools merged for middle and high school, I had already learned how to go unnoticed. I was thin and small and didn't really hit my growth spurt until the summer after my sophomore year. But I had all the tricks down. Never speak in class unless called on, which I tried to avoid at all costs. Don't make eye contact. Look busy writing down notes when the teacher calls on you. Volunteer for things that don't require you to speak, like working out a math problem on the board. And, if by chance, I did get called on, I'd hear the voices of various speech therapists I'd had through the years saying, "Slow down, relax, then give it a try." Every once in a while, a teacher realized I was struggling to get the words out, and he or she would finish the sentence for me, but with any luck, I was able to get it out with minimal embarrassment.

Sometime after I settled in at St. Xavier, I stopped caring as much about the stutter. I made some friends through running, and Margot stopped noticing it long ago.

But then my thoughts shift to how strange it is to feel so lost in such a familiar space. The peeling purple border of the health class bulletin board next to where I stand was something that I passed every day and hadn't changed in years. The laminated food pyramid poster hangs next to another poster that reads "You are what you eat" with pictures of two boys standing next to each other. One has Pop-Tarts shoulders and French fry hair, while the other one's hair is broccoli on a carrot stick neck. I've always kind of loved the Pop-Tarts shoulder guy. I lean back, try to get my bearings.

I watch Mrs. Montgomery stick her head out of her classroom to yell at two boys dribbling a ball back and forth and begin to search the crowd for Margot again when I hear Gabriella's cheerful voice say, "There you are."

I turn to face her and force myself to return her smile with a small, shaky one.

"Hey," I say, digging my hands in my pockets.

"What are you doing?" she asks.

"I really don't know what I'm doing," I say, looking down at the floor as everything continues to bustle around me. "I was outside, but then it felt like I should be in here . . ." My voice trails off at the end of my sentence.

"I've been keeping an eye on you out there, just so you know," she says. "You've been doing a lot of sleeping with the numbing. I just came to find you because we thought at this point you might be up to walking around for a while." I stare at her and shift my stance from one leg to another, trying to decide whether or not to ask her why she's monitoring me.

Before I make up my mind she says, "Come on. Let us fill you in on some more stuff."

"Yeah, that's fine." I nod. "Question though: what's the deal with these guys again?" I ask, pointing over at the pale figures causing the water fountain to go on and off.

"Oh, these guys?" she says, reaching out and swatting a hand right through them. They don't respond at all. She smiles at me. "They're harmless. Just leftover energy. You'll see them all over the place, but they come and go. Nobody who's alive can see them. Well, usually . . ." she smiles and raises her eyebrows. "They're not just here, in this school. They were all around you when you were alive. But like I said, they're usually harmless."

I'm about to ask what she means by "usually" when she continues, "Come on. Let's go find Stewart."

She leads me down the hallway. I feel a sudden pang of distress, but it comes and goes like the annoyance of a bug bite. Gabriella continues to charge a path towards the gym where the freshman first period PE classes are gathering in loud groups waiting for instruction. She raises her voice to compete with them.

"So as you probably know, being a much more current student than us, this little lounge outside the gym doesn't get much use. When they built the one off the cafeteria, that became more of the spot." She shrugs. A basketball whizzes by a few inches in front of my face. I flinch and she smiles. "But that's good for us. It makes it a lot easier."

"Okay," I say. I feel obligated to let her know I'm following along, even though I am not sure what she means.

"Oh, you probably noticed," she continues as we approach the double doors at the end of the gym, "that you'll interact with objects however you will yourself to. So even though you can choose to push on this handle and open the door, make sure you don't do that during school hours." She motions her head towards the students. "We try not to freak them out, basically."

"Got it," I say and follow her lead of walking through the closed doors.

Stewart greets us on the other side. Next to him stands Ali Townsend, who widens her eyes at me and gives a little wave. I wave back at her, trying to make sense of the strained expression on her face.

"Hey man," Stewart says, lifting his chin towards me. "How ya feeling?"

"Good," I shrug.

"Groggy," says Gabriella. Stewart nods.

"Yeah, I think I've been out here like maybe once," I say, squinting and looking around. "I sort of forgot it was here."

"Most of the students have, I think," says Stewart. "I mean, some haven't, and they use it as a hideout spot, but for the most part, it's really quiet out here. Which is good for us."

"Do we need lots of quiet or something?" I ask, shifting my eyes back and forth between all of them. Come to think of it, what are my basic needs right now, now that they are no longer food, water, and sleep?

"No," Gabriella shrugs. "But it's definitely nice sometimes."

A small gust of wind blows some dead leaves into a corner, and we all turn our heads in the direction of the crackling.

"It's more like they don't get in the way of what we need out here," Stewart says, kneeling down and wiping his hand over a dirty spot on a brick.

I look around at the space. It looks neglected. Four cement walls are streaked with graffiti—Sharpie-stained elaborate cursive writing or big basic lettering, occasionally a small drawing, most of it in black, but sometimes a purple or dark green. But the drab grayness of the place reminds me of a rainy day at the beach. I understand why nobody uses it.

"So, you might be wondering," says Gabriella, "how we know everything we know." Before I have a chance to respond, Stewart jumps in.

"A lot of the info is passed down," Stewart says, walking towards one corner. He kneels down and rubs his hand along a section of the wall. "But really, this is the stuff that's important. We get almost everything we need to know from the graffiti."

My eyes narrow as I take in all the scribbling.

"We get a lot of messages through it," says Gabriella, watching me.

"We spend a lot of time out here," Stewart adds, standing and spreading his arms around. "In case there is ever something new that we need to know. Someone we need to help." He pauses. "It's okay if it doesn't make sense to you yet. It will."

"Graffiti?" I ask, looking up and catching Ali staring at me.

"I'll be going over all of this more in the next couple of days with you, James, now that the numbing has kicked in. But the missions, your missions, are why you are here," Stewart adds.

"You're here to help them," Ali says flatly.

I feel exhaustion start to jab at my body like a boxer trying to get a feel for his opponent. "I sort of remember you telling me some of this," I say. "Listen, I'm sorry, I think I need to sit for a minute." I walk to the nearest part of the stone wall, where Ali is standing, and slink down.

"Of course," says Stewart. "Just relax if you need to."

"The numbing," Gabriella adds. "It'll come and go like that for a while."

Ali sits down next to me and pats my shoulder.

"Tell me again," I say, closing my eyes and leaning my head back. "Why are we here? We're like guardian angels or something?" I think of Margot, but I know that I don't have the energy to continue looking for her right now.

"You ever watch one of those nature documentaries on TV?" Stewart asks. My eyes flutter open. "You know how sometimes, even though you know it's just nature, you want to jump in and save the zebra from the lion? Well, that's what we do. Every once in a while we save the zebra."

"How do you know when you're supposed to save the zebra and when you're not?" I ask. Ali sighs.

"Like when should you just let nature take its course?" asks Gabriella. I look at her, heavy-eyed, and nod. "Because that's why we're here. That's our purpose, James. If you see it, and it bothers you enough that you feel inclined to help them somehow, then you should help. There's negative energy out there constantly trying to attach itself to them. Sometimes it does. Sometimes it should. But sometimes it's too much and they just need the scales tipped back in their favor for a bit. So, we're kind of like scale tippers."

"We're silent interferers," Stewart says from the other corner.

"We're dead," I say. "And we're here, but we're not really here. We're . . . ghosts. We're ghosts."

"Here," Ali says, standing. "Let me help you up. I'll show you some of the graffiti." She holds out her hands to me, and I groan a little before taking them and standing. Then she leans in and whispers, "You don't have to be here. You can leave." I give her a confused look, and she holds a finger up to her lips and mouths, "Shh."

Margot

"Be there soon."

It takes five days before she is able to look at her phone and see that final text. When she looks at it, she sucks in a deep breath and thoughts of the red plastic chairs at the coffee shop and the smell of James' latte flash through her mind.

There is one voicemail from him, and the familiarity of his voice is comforting and agonizing. "Margot, Margot, Margot . . . Call me back!" She replays it over and over again and wonders how it's possible that he can be gone when his voice is right there, sounding so young and immediate.

On the eighth day her mother insists that she come with her to see the Therioults and drop off a meal to them.

"Let them comfort you, Margot, and you comfort them," she says. "You don't have to stay long."

"Mom, I love the Therioults, but I am not sure I can be in that house. I just . . ."

"You can."

Her mother does not meet her eyes and is covering up a glass baking dish on the counter with aluminum foil.

"You can," she repeats without turning around. "And you should. It's the right thing to do."

Margot shakes her head and sputters with her mouth open.

"It's going to be hard. But you can do it," her mother continues.

Margot does not speak on the way over there and her hands are shaking as they approach the side door to the kitchen. She hears his voice, "Margot, Margot, Margot . . . Call me back!" and her eyes begin to brim with tears.

"Mom, I—" she starts, but the door opens and before she can get any more words out, Mrs. Therioult is out on the porch with her arms wrapped around her, swaying back and forth.

"I'm so glad you came," she whispers as she buries her head in Margot's hair. Margot snuffles and then tears come as she says, "He loved you so much, Margot."

"I'm sorry," she manages to choke out. "I'm really sorry."

"Patricia, I'm going to go in and put this on the counter," Margot's mother says softly after a few moments.

His mom takes her hand and leads Margot into the kitchen. The white stone counters look empty but for a clump of crumbs by the toaster. James' dad rounds the corner. His hair is messy and his eyes look tired.

"Margot," he says and stops in his tracks.

"Hi," she manages.

"We've been thinking of you," he says and puts his hand on her shoulder.

"Thank you," she mouths, feeling stupid that they are consoling her.

"Margot's just now feeling up to leaving the house," her mother chimes in from the other side of the kitchen. "You've both been in her prayers."

James' dad nods. Their black lab enters the kitchen, his toenails clacking on the tile.

"Bear!" she exclaims, dropping to her knees as he wags his tail slowly and approaches. She remembers James as a boy dancing around the room with him. At that time the dog on his hind legs had been nearly as tall as he was. Now he takes small, stiff steps, and white covers his face like a dusting of snow.

"Bear's as lost as we all are, I think," says his dad. She strokes the dog's silky ears for a moment and then stands up.

"I'm so sorry I didn't come," she says, meeting his mother's eyes. "I should have. And I'm really sorry." Her lip quivers.

"It's okay darlin'," Mrs. Therioult replies, her eyes glassy. "We know you would have been there if you were able." Her voice cracks.

"We're all just getting by the best we can," his dad adds. "There's no playbook for your heart breaking."

"Have you all eaten?" Margot's mother asks. "I can heat this up. It's just a little lasagna."

"No, we hadn't gotten around to dinner yet. That sounds nice," his mother replies.

In the mudroom around the corner, Margot spots a pair of James' orange Adidas sneakers and sucks in her breath. She hears his voice complaining about the hole in the bottom of them when he stepped in a puddle. That seems like just days ago. How are they there without him?

The tears come without her realizing it at first. She feels all of them around her, embracing her.

Finally, her mother suggests, "Why don't I set the table and we can all sit down together for a little while."

When they gather around the dining room table, Bear sits on her feet while they hold hands and his dad says, "Bless us, Lord, as we all struggle to find our way with heavy hearts. May we continue to find comfort in happy memories." Margot stares hard at the familiar blue and white wallpaper and concentrates on not crying anymore as he speaks.

They begin to eat and for a few minutes, there is only the sound of the utensils hitting the plate.

"Margot, you know what I was thinking about the other day?" James' mom says with a smile. "Remember when y'all made that lemonade stand? And that little table collapsed?"

Margot finishes chewing a bite of her lasagna and says, "Yes. And we were covered with lemonade, and James got stung by a wasp. It was not a good day."

"Oh, I forgot about that sting! He was so upset."

His dad clears his throat and takes a sip of wine.

"Well," says Margot's mother, "I was smiling the other day remembering how much he liked that airplane-shaped swing at the park as a little guy. His tiny little legs would bolt right to it the second you got them out of the car. Margot, you loved the ladybug seesaw and you'd just sit on one end of it calling his name until he came and joined you."

"He really did love that swing," Margot says, pushing a piece of lasagna around. She had been losing her appetite for a while, even before she lost James.

It feels good to talk about him, to reminisce sweetly about him instead of sitting in her room avoiding everything, crying. Her posture relaxes and she allows the smile to stay on her face for a little while between bites.

Maybe it is easier to talk about memories of child James. That way they didn't have to remember the version of him that was ripped away from them, just the version of him that was a sweet picture in their memories anyway.

Her eyes feel heavy. She may have taken more than she should have this time. She nods off for a split second. Her chin drops and her fork hits the side of her plate with a clang. She glances around the table. Nobody seems to have noticed.

She thinks about the playground, and she remembers his eyes watching her from that swing that he loved while she waited for him to join her on the seesaw. And then she remembers how he always did.

James

Ali's words keep coming back to me as I sit at the main entrance. I want to find her and ask her more, but right now I'm sitting on the twenty-sixth step. It's where I waited for Margot every morning when I was alive. I would have picked her up and driven her with me, but Margot's mother is a control freak. So every morning I waited here.

When I first started at St. Xavier, it took me a while to figure out just where in the huge walkway was the perfect waiting spot—not too close to the bottom to look anxious and not too close to the crowded doorway.

I see Ali come through the doors. She looks annoyed as she weaves between the crowds to take her usual spot underneath the massive oak tree next to the school. She seems to spend a lot of time there by herself. I'm thinking about how I can get out there to talk to her alone when I hear a car horn.

I look up to see the Cramer family Volvo cutting off a school bus. I rise, anxiety tingling my senses. She's back. It's taken eleven school days, but finally, here she is.

At first, she is a slumped figure in the passenger seat. Her mother reaches over and puts a hand on her back. I see her shake her head several times and then reach in slow motion to the back seat to retrieve her backpack. Finally, she gets out of the car.

She walks with her head down. I'm straining to see her face, but when she tucks a strand of hair behind an ear, I notice that she seems to be talking to herself. I freeze as she gets closer, and when she pauses on the twenty-sixth step, swallows hard, and continues into school, I realize that she has been counting.

I rush in the door ahead of her so that she's walking towards me, and I can get a good look at her.

Her usually pin-straight strawberry blonde hair falls all around her face, and her white uniform shirt and plaid skirt are wrinkled.

There are a few soft calls of "Hey Margot," and Virginia Stanley even goes so far as to say, "Good to have you back, Margot," but everyone seems to back away from her.

She makes her way to her locker. I can't believe that I have not noticed until now that it is still covered in wrapping paper from when me and Kimberley decorated it for her birthday a few weeks ago. I wish someone had taken it down. It seems so stupidly cheerful right now.

She has to check back in with the school secretary before heading to homeroom, a St. Xavier rule if you've been absent, so she continues her slow walk from her locker to the office, where Sister Ellen is sprawled out behind a massive desk. She reminds me of a walrus on an island of busy penguins. Margot waits in the slow-moving line of students until it is her turn.

"I need to sign in after being absent," she says.

"Name?" Sister Ellen asks without looking up from the big ledger-style book that she keeps on her desk, which is apparently the master record of when every student has been sick or left early for a doctor's appointment. I think one of the other office helpers inputs the list into the school database at the end of the day. There are definitely more efficient ways of doing things, but technology and Sister Ellen are not acquainted.

"Margot Cramer."

"Oh, Margot honey," she says, looking up and then lowering her voice. "Where's your mother?"

"I wanted to walk in by myself."

Sister Ellen pauses and then pushes up the glasses that have slipped to the bottom of her nose. "Okay, honey. Well, Mrs. Burns would like to see you before you head to your homeroom. Pop in there real quick before you go. I'll mark down any tardies this morning as excused." She looks back down at the book and begins writing.

"Do I have to?"

"What's that, honey?" she replies, pen scrawling across the page.

"Do I have to go see Mrs. Burns? I mean, I really don't want to."

"She just wants to make sure that you're okay, dear."

"Well, I'm not okay." I think I see her hands tremble as she places them down to lean on the desk. "But I am here. And I really just want to go to my homeroom."

"I think it's probably a good idea to check in with her first, Margot."

This comes out as more direct than stern.

"So is this mandatory or suggested?" Margot's voice starts to rise.

"Honey, she just wants to make sure—"

"Of what?" Margot yells. The office goes silent around her.

"Your mother thought it would be a good idea too," Sister Ellen says, leaning towards Margot and lowering her voice. But Margot is not taking any cues from Sister Ellen's volume.

"I don't care!" she shouts. "I just want to go to my class!"

Mrs. Burns comes flying out of her office and puts a hand on Margot's shoulder while whispering furiously in her ear. I can see the strain on Margot's face. She looks like she is trying hard not to cry, and I can't stand how on display she is. She doesn't deserve everyone looking at her right now.

I swipe at the first thing I see, which happens to be a ceramic paperweight on Sister Ellen's desk. It crashes to the ground, and all heads turn away from Margot to look at the remnants.

"Now how did that happen?" Sister Ellen wonders, sticking her head around her desk as Mrs. Burns shuffles Margot out.

"Be careful with that." I spin around to find Gabriella leaning against the doorway to the main office. "It can weird them out."

I rub my forehead as Sister Ellen comes around to sweep the mess up off the floor. She groans as she twists into different positions to get the shards.

"I didn't really mean to. It was just hard to see her so upset and have everyone staring at her."

"I get it. So, that's Margot, huh?"

I nod and stare towards Mrs. Burns' closed doors.

"You can always go in and listen," Gabriella says, tilting her chin in that same direction.

"I don't think I can do that."

She shrugs. "It can be hard to figure out the boundaries sometimes, but you will."

I nod at her, but I'm barely listening. I see the closed doors. All I can think about is breaking them down.

Margot

"What happened out there?" Mrs. Burns pulls a chair right up in front of her. She places both hands on Margot's arms, but Margot just shakes her head and continues to cry. Tears drip into her lap and sit on the uniform skirt for a moment before eventually sinking into the fabric.

"Margot . . ."

"I just want to go to class! I just want to go right to my class and sit down and open my book and not have to talk to anyone."

"I can understand feeling that way, but—"

"And then Sister Ellen kept saying I *had* to go to you. I *had* to go to you. And I kept telling her that I really didn't want to, but she kept insisting!"

"I'm sorry. I'm very sorry, Margot. Your mother and I thought that it was possible you might need a few minutes to gather yourself after coming back for the first time. That it might have been hard to walk through the door and go directly to class. We thought that if we had you check in with me then you would be able to sit for a few minutes if you needed to."

"I didn't need to."

"And Sister Ellen was just trying to be helpful."

"Well, she wasn't."

"I understand." Mrs. Burns sits back in her chair. They stay silent for a moment.

"Are you ready to be here, Margot? Do you think that you can do this?"

"It's not like I can just stay at home for the rest of my life."

"Well, that is true. But I'm not talking about the rest of

your life. I'm talking about a stretch of time if you are not ready."

"What I wasn't ready for is what happened to James." Her bottom lip trembles and more tears begin to drip down her cheeks. Mrs. Burns has to swallow hard to stay strong for the girl. Her grief is palpable, a scent that overpowers the room.

"Of course not. Nobody could ever truly be ready for something so difficult." There was a long silence. "What feels right for you right now, Margot?"

Margot shrugs. Stares at the wall. "I'm here, aren't I?"

"Do you want some time in here to regroup before going to class? I can even leave you alone if you'd like."

"I just want to go to class. It's just like I told Sister Ellen," she closes her eyes and whispers with exasperation.

"Okay." Mrs. Burns nods. "Would you like me to walk with you there?"

"No, thank you," Margot answers, standing up and grabbing her backpack from its landing spot, where she had hurled it upon entering the office.

James flinches as the door to the office swings open, bashing the wall behind it, where he's been waiting. Gabriella giggles.

"It's hard to remember that nothing can hurt you now, isn't it?" But James does not reply. Instead, he follows Margot down the hallway.

She is walking with determined anger. The hallway is silent since classes started ten minutes ago. The only sound is that of the rubber soles of her shoes hitting the tile floor.

Margot doesn't pause at all before entering Mr. McAdams' history class. In fact, James is surprised at how she just whips open the door and walks right in. Mr. McAdams' body is turned toward the board, and without looking up from what he is writing, he says, "You're late."

Since there comes no apology, he turns partially around and sees the girl making a beeline for the first empty desk. Margot Cramer. The one that was friends with the Therioult boy. The one that they thought would never come back.

James closes his eyes and hopes that Mr. McAdams will let it slide. It is bad enough that she has every eye in the room on her. Instead, he says, "I'm sure you were checking in with the office, Miss Cramer. Please get settled."

There is something about the familiar hardness of the chair and the sound of the zipper on her backpack, the horrible squeak when someone slides their desk around, that makes Margot feel at ease. She thrusts her chin forward and focuses on the board, a stoic look on her face despite the red, blotchy skin and the puffy eyes. James smiles.

"There she is," he thinks.

She feels her hands shaking. That has been getting worse lately. She sits on them.

James

I am restless on the bleachers that night. It still feels like hours before the sun will come up. I get up and head towards the school, feeling fog start to form around me as I walk. Maybe if I stayed with the others in the lounge at night I wouldn't feel as lonely as I do right now, but I'm still not entirely sure about them, and I don't want constant companionship.

I decide maybe the library would be a good place to kill some time as I pass through the doors. I glance up at the clock on the wall. 4:10 am. Suddenly I hear low musical notes that start to thread themselves together into a sad song. I follow the sound down the hallway towards the music room and peek in to see Ali playing a cello, a look of concentration painted across her face as she stares at music on a black stand.

I wonder if I should leave her alone, but I need to find out what she meant about being able to leave and something about Margot's return is making me feel lonely. I decide to go in and wait until she's done, but she notices me right away and lets the bow slide off the instrument and down to her side.

"Hi," she says, a confused look on her face.

"Hi. I'm sorry. I heard the music, so I followed it."

"It's okay. I hope I didn't disturb you. I like to try to get some practice in every day, and Mr. Mitchell comes early and stays late so I have to work around him. I think his wife drives him crazy." She smiles.

"No, you didn't disturb me at all."

"Oh good."

"Couldn't really relax, so I decided to just walk around. It was nice. What you were playing, I mean."

"Thanks." She closes the music book on the stand. "So are you doing okay? I'm sorry I haven't really been around to help you more. I figured the other two were still swarming around you. They're nice and all, but

I guess I just prefer to do my own thing." She shrugs.

"I get it." We lock eyes. She looks away.

"Also, I know that numbing crap can knock you out, so I was giving you some time. But you're feeling okay?"

"Yeah. Yeah, I mean I *feel* okay . . ."

"But it's all just super bizarre?"

I nod. "Today I saw my girlfriend for the first time, and . . ." She tilts her head at me, waiting for me to finish. "It was just tough."

"I understand. I had pissed off most of my good friends before I died, but still it was hard to see them at first. It should get easier."

"Yeah." I sigh. "That's what I'm told."

"But you don't really believe it? I'm just guessing by the look on your face." She smiles.

"I believe it. I mean, I don't think anyone has a reason to lie to me."

"Let me ask you something, James," she says, turning her head away from me and tightening the strings on the cello. "Do you hear them?"

"Who?"

She stares at me, reading my facial expression.

"I guess you don't." She goes back to tuning the cello.

"Hear what?" I ask over the music. "And also, what did you mean outside? When you said I don't have to stay here?"

She glances up at the clock and then at the door. "I should probably start packing up. Feel like taking a walk with me?"

"Sure." I wait as she delicately carries the cello to the closet and puts everything away.

"I have my own type of mission," she says as she leads the way down the hall and I follow. She ducks into the teachers' lounge.

I stare as she slams shut one of the flimsy, cream-colored cabinets by the sink. Looking at the door behind me, she asks, "Can you stick your head out and tell me if you see any teachers?"

I pop out and back in and then I shake my head at her. "Nothing. Why?"

"Changing the coffee."

I stare at her with a confused look on my face, which she ignores as she reaches for a white coffee filter.

"Can I ask why?"

"Sure," she says and fills the machine with water. "Mr. Johnson is usually the first one in here to get his coffee." She fiddles with the glass pot on the burner. "Before my memorial service started, I heard him whisper to Mr. Franklin that I basically deserved what I got. So, whenever I remember, I come in here and put decaf coffee in the pot instead of regular. Among other things . . ."

She turns around and smiles at me as the machine clicks on. It sputters as it begins to drip hot coffee into the pot.

"I get it." I smile back at her.

"Now let's get out of here."

"Ali?"

"Yes?"

"What did you mean when you said I could leave?"

She folds her arms, glances around the room, and then meets my eyes.

"I meant that you don't have to stay here. And I am the only one who will tell you that."

Margot

She would never admit it, but Margot has been using her "tools" from Mrs. Burns—the slow, deliberate breathing from her diaphragm, the affirmations and redirecting of thoughts. For the last few days, they have been enough to allow her to function. Normalcy is beginning to feel like a foggy day that you keep walking through with only the belief that there is something on the other side. She is getting better at going through the motions. Except on her fourth day back, when she needs a pencil.

Geometry test. She is ready. She just needs to get through it and it will be lunchtime. She will try to get to the cafeteria before Amanda spots her, grab one of the prewrapped ham and cheese sandwiches, pick off the ham, and take it outside to eat in solitude. She can't stand the thought of sitting at the hard brown tables in the loud cafeteria, full of people laughing and yelling and being stupid. Kimberley and Jennifer will be waiting for her by her locker after this class, and for a moment she feels badly thinking of them wasting their time there, being late for lunch. But she just can't explain herself today. Can't sit and listen to weekend plans and act interested in stupid gossip when all she wants to do is scream inside.

She leans over the side of her desk to root around in her backpack for a number 2 pencil that isn't broken. When her hand emerges from the bag, she notices that she is holding a green pencil that James had lent her one day. She stares, twirling it around in her fingers. He had chewed on it, and something about the impression of his teeth in the wood makes her unravel.

Her heart races. Her cheeks flush. She jumps up from her desk, still holding the pencil. Heads swivel to find the source of the commotion. Without meeting any eyes, she swallows hard, scoops up her backpack, and exits through the back door of the classroom as murmurs begin and the teacher looks up from the desk.

She considers for a moment going to see Mrs. Burns, not because she needs the comfort of her words, but more for the seclusion that her office provides. But the stress of having to walk by Sister Ellen after her outburst on the first day back is an embarrassment that she isn't up for.

She decides to head to the library instead. It is easy enough to hide there. She'll enlist Mrs. Burns' help later in being officially excused from math.

James keeps pace behind her. He had been walking towards the classroom to sit near her when he saw her burst out of the geometry classroom. Her shoulders are slumped and her expression looks strained, as if the slightest easing of facial muscles will result in a barrage of tears. She drops a pencil on the ground in the hallway. James scoops it up and puts it in his pocket.

He follows closely behind her. Her quick footsteps become muffled once they transition from the hallway into the gray institutional carpeting of the library, but her skirt continues to swoosh with her pace as she makes her way towards one of the partitioned workstations in the back of the room. When she reaches a free one, she immediately buries her face in her arms and begins to cry.

The crying itself is silent, but her shoulders rise and fall. James hovers over her, holds his own face in his hands, and rubs his eyes. He can smell the familiar flowery scent of her shampoo.

"It's called study hall, not sleep hall," says a voice from behind them. Father Gary is passing through, checking on students in this back section. He has a booming voice that he has managed to tone down for the library, and with his usual dignified posture, he glides toward her. "Young lady, if you are in here for a study hall then you are to be working."

Margot snuffles as she draws her head up. She nods at him and forces a weak smile.

"Sorry, Father, I just wasn't feeling very well for a moment."

He pauses, stares hard at her, and then nods as he continues his rounds.

She tucks her hair behind her ears, wipes at her eyes, and squares her shoulders.

"I am sad, but I am going to be okay," she repeats in her head. She draws a slow breath in from the pit of her stomach that elongates her spine before closing her eyes and exhaling.

She pushes the chair back and then stands. Maybe if she can find a book to get absorbed in it will be enough to redirect her thoughts for the afternoon. She moves towards the fiction section with slow, deliberate steps as if she is unsure of her exact destination. She wanders around near the entrance of the aisles.

FA-FR. She touches the laminated sign at the beginning of the faded wooden bookcases. James watches her from a distance, wondering if his suspicion is correct.

Margot had been obsessed with *The Great Gatsby* in eighth grade when her honors English course spent the better part of a semester dissecting it. It led to a long stretch of her treating the novel like a Magic 8-ball for decision making or advice. She'd flip to random pages and extract meaning from whatever line in the book her finger would land on.

There is a crash as the seat at Margot's workstation falls to the ground from the weight of her backpack. She jumps and then sighs at the sight of papers scattered on the floor and pencils and pens rolling everywhere.

James has an idea and he needs to move quickly. He glances around to see if there is anyone else in the vicinity of the F section, and when he sees that there isn't, he flies to the Fitzgerald books. He looks back at Margot, still working on picking up her things, grabs the book, and puts it on the floor.

He looks up again. There's nobody around to notice the pages moving.

"C'mon," he thinks. "Give me something good!" He flips and scans, flips and scans. And then he smiles, takes the green pencil he is still carrying, and underlines something.

Margot is just finishing with her backpack mess. He sticks the pencil in the page that he has underlined and jams the book back on the shelf. Then he stands and watches her.

"Please come back," he thinks.

After taking great care to position her backpack on the desk this time instead of the chair, she begins to take steps back toward the shelf.

"Come on . . . ," James whispers.

And she does. She looks all around her as if she is conducting some sort of secretive action and then darts into the aisle. She scans the Fs with her finger until she finds the book and pulls it off the shelf.

James watches as her brow furrows and she holds the book closer, balancing it on her stomach as she opens it to remove the pencil. Her eyes widen as she fingers the pencil and then reads the underlined words.

"She was feeling the pressure of the world outside and she wanted to see him and feel his presence beside her and be reassured that she was doing the right thing after all."

She drops the book to the ground, mouth open. Short, nervous breaths escape from her as she scans her eyes from side to side.

He smiles.

James

I'm waiting on the twenty-sixth step and thinking about what Ali told me. I don't have to stay here. There are ways out. "There is even a way back," she whispered, studying my face hard and then saying, "They will tell you that's not possible. But it is." Something about the intensity in her eyes threw me off. Then Stewart walked in, and she stopped talking. My mind has been a cesspool of curiosity and doubt and trust issues ever since.

The crowd of students starts to become a slow trickle. I must have missed Margot. When the first-period bell rings, I remember I am supposed to meet up with everyone in the teachers' lounge. I'll have to catch up with Margot later.

I bump into Stewart on the way there, and we walk together.

"It's so weird to know that you were here watching us this whole time," I say to Stewart.

"Good weird or bad weird?" he asks.

"A little of both, I guess. Just weird that they have no clue." I motion towards a group waiting outside their science class.

He nods. "It's for the best. Imagine how freaked out they'd be if they did know."

"Yeah," I mumble and look down at my feet.

"Besides," he says, "watch this." He approaches one of the kids in the group and touches his shoulder. The boy reaches his hand up and starts scratching where Stewart touched. He watches me and does it again. Same reaction. "We make them itchy." He smiles.

"Really? All of them?"

"All of them," he answers, touching a girl on a different shoulder. Her hand shoots up and claws at the spot.

"Why?"

He shrugs. "Don't really know. I guess we mess with their energy or something."

"Let me try," I say, touching another guy on his back. It takes a minute, but his hand drifts up to scratch the spot. I look over at Stewart and he nods.

"Come on," he says and laughs.

We follow Mrs. Garcia into the teachers' lounge. I am so close to her that I can see dandruff that has fallen on the shoulders of her blouse. She strolls in and puts her coffee cup in the microwave. Gabriella also slips in through the open door, followed by Ali.

"Have a seat," says Stewart, motioning towards the Formica table in the middle of the room. As we sit, I look around at the pale yellow walls, splattered with printed announcements or remnants of old tape where previous ones had been hung.

Mr. Cohen, a math teacher, is sitting at the end of the long table reading a newspaper and drinking coffee. His glass clinks down on the tabletop as he raises the cup to his lips and then puts it back down again without moving his eyes from the paper.

From the other corner of the lounge, the microwave beeps and Mrs. Garcia clears her throat. Mr. Cohen looks up at her and says, "Oh Elena, didn't hear you come in. How have you been?"

She clears her throat again, making the phlegm rattle around. "This darn cold. I can't get rid of it."

"I know, this place is like a germ factory sometimes," he replies, shaking his head.

"So this is kind of why we're here, James," Stewart says. "The teachers talk a lot in here. It can give us good ideas about some of the kids that we need to look out for. The ones that might be a little more susceptible to other forces."

"Other forces?" I ask.

"Well, just having a hard time," Stewart replies.

"It's just good to be aware of fluctuations," says Gabriella. "To stay somewhat connected to them, know who they are and all that." I look over at Ali and she raises her eyebrows at me.

"Not much this morning though," Stewart adds. "And these two are just talking about the weather. We hear a lot of that."

"Biggest rush is about 7:45 when they're all getting their coffee before first period," Gabriella says.

A noise from the corner makes us all turn our heads. A residual, like the watery figures I saw on the football field and messing with the water fountain, this one an older figure that appears to be a teacher, rises from an armchair and lights a pipe before going through the wall.

"We call him Dan," Gabriella says. "He's in here like clockwork every morning around this time."

"Did somebody leave an empty coffee pot on the burner again?" Mrs. Garcia asks Mr. Cohen. "It smells like something is smoking." She walks over towards the coffee machine.

"Really?" he says, sniffing the air. "I'm not getting it."

They all smile as puffs of Dan's smoke evaporate. "I have to admit, I do love it when stuff like that happens," says Ali.

"So nothing here this morning, but has everybody checked their graffiti? I was thinking we could show James how to retrieve a mission."

Ali looks down at her feet. "I still haven't become comfortable with that yet, Stewart," she mumbles.

"I'm not asking you to act on it, but it might be good just to check and see if anything jumps out at you in the writing. There may be kids that need you to affect them somehow and you don't even know it."

"Nobody's waiting on me."

"You don't know that though, Ali. That's the problem." Gabriella crosses her arms and looks at Stewart, widening her eyes.

"It's just the way I feel. I can't explain it."

"We're going to be showing James anyway, so why don't you just walk out with us?"

Ali shakes her head and shrugs. "Fine."

My eyes dart between them. I want out of the teachers' lounge, and I don't want to go look at graffiti. I've already missed Margot's arrival and part of first period.

"Alright James, let's see if you're ready to receive a mission," Stewart says, standing up and clapping his hands together.

I look at Ali as we all stand, and she rolls her eyes at me. I give her a little nod, but I follow Stewart. I'm still not sure who has the right directions for the way out, but I know I'm going to need some sort of map.

Margot

The stench of the formaldehyde hits Margot the moment she opens the door, and she gasps a little. A few heads turn her way and then go back to their group conversations. Katie and Kimberley wave to her from the corner of the biology classroom. She is about to make her way over to them, but Mrs. Farley is coming in the door right behind her and says, "Find an open seat quickly so we can get started please." Crap, how could she have forgotten about frog dissection day?

She walks toward the only empty stool that she sees at one of the lab tables and tries to size up her partner as she reaches into her bag for her binder. Is Douglas his name? He dated that girl that OD'd. He stares down at his hands, picking at calluses, and sometimes glancing up at Mrs. Farley as she rattles off the rules of the dissection lab again.

"You want me to get the tray?" he asks, startling Margot out of the place she had drifted off to.

"Oh, um yeah. That would be great. Thanks." He smiles and nods, running a hand through his hair as he turns to walk away, returning a few minutes later and plunking down a silver tray between them.

"Umm, okay," Margot says with fake confidence in her voice. "Do you want to do the first incision then?"

He laughs and shrugs. "Uh, I can. Unless you wanted to do it?"

"I actually don't think I want to do any of it!" Margot cringes and then looks up at him. The frog lays splayed out between them. He does an impromptu imitation of it and they both start giggling. It is the first genuine smile she feels cross her face in some time.

"Seriously though, I am really not sure I can do this." Margot's smile recedes, and she stares down at the tray again.

"Farley did say that if anyone's uncomfortable to just let her know."

"I know. I don't really want to get a bad grade though. I still have a lot of makeup work from when I was out for a while."

"I got it," he says, picking up the scalpel and twisting it around before he steadies it in his hands.

"Thank you. God, the smell is making me nauseous."

"Yeah, it's gross. I'm probably going to need some help labeling the parts though. I didn't really memorize them like we were supposed to."

"Okay. If I don't vomit first."

"Alright, let's go ahead and get this over with," he says, sighing. His pale hand turns pink as it grips the scalpel and then he lowers it to make the first incision. Margot winces and turns her head.

"I guess you're not going to be working toward medical school?"

"No, definitely not my thing," she says, forcing herself to turn her head back towards the tray.

"Well, what is your thing then? And what's this thing?" he points the tip of his pencil toward a frog organ that matches up with the picture on his worksheet.

Margot glances toward the table and then at the windows in the back of the classroom. "It's the stomach," she says. "And I don't really have a thing," Margot continues while Douglas scribbles "stomach" on his diagram.

"Everyone has a thing," he says.

"I like writing, I guess. I don't know. What's yours?"

"Um, drums. What's this little thing?"

"Spleen. Drums? Are you in a band or anything?"

"No. My dad took them away last year, so I don't really get to play. And this thing?"

"Pancreas. Why did your dad take them away?"

"Long story. You know, if you can get past the grossness, this is really kind of amazing."

"Douglas, Margot, you're doing alright?" Mrs. Farley asks

as she approaches their table. They nod and she moves on. They are quiet as he pauses to make some notes on his paper.

"So what happened with your drums?"

"What?" he asks, a surprised look on his face before he begins to poke at the frog some more.

"Your drums." He narrows his eyes as she stares at him. "Whatever, sorry. It's none of my business."

He nods and starts to doodle on the edge of his sheet. A few minutes go by and Margot says, "I think we can probably just figure the last few out by process of elimination."

"Oh yeah, sorry. Was kind of zoning." He flicks his hair to the side and flashes a nervous smile but something about his eyes looks sad.

Mrs. Farley bellows, "Alright people, let's wrap it up and commence with the cleanup!" Margot hesitates, but Douglas springs up and follows the lead of the others in the class.

"Please make sure that you get together with your partner before the next class and write a summary of your dissection experience. Make sure you touch on all the points that are on the sheet I emailed. See you Monday!" calls Mrs. Farley over the rising volume of her students.

"My weekend's pretty busy," Douglas says as he returns to the table. "Mind if we try and knock this out today? Probably will be easier while it's fresh on the mind anyway."

"Sure." Margot shrugs.

"Meet at PJ's after school real quick?"

"No, not a coffee shop, please," she says, closing her eyes.

She's pretty, he thinks, taking a good look at her now. He didn't notice how pretty she was at the table. "Oh, um, alright. Library okay?"

She nods. "What time?"

"How about right after school? I have some stuff to get to later."

"See you there." She watches as he leaves and sighs. It's going to mean she can't get back to her bedroom as quickly as she likes to after school, but for the first time in a while, the thought of it doesn't make her want to scream.

James

I swallow hard as we walk through the gym doors to the outside lounge. The bell just rang between periods, and I am trying to remember where Margot is now. Biology? I can't stop thinking about her reaction to the book, and I'm desperate to see her.

"Does that make sense?" Gabriella says to me as we enter into the sunlight. Ali looks over at me and raises her eyebrows.

"I'm sorry. I was kind of distracted for a minute." I catch Ali smiling at me now, but she looks away when Gabriella glances over at her. Stewart is on his knees by one section of the wall, tilting his head at it.

"What I was saying was that it looks different for everyone," Gabriella starts. "You will know it's your graffiti because it will speak to you somehow. I just can't tell you how."

"Mine usually glows for me a little," Stewart says, now running his hand over the concrete.

"Mine flashes," Gabriella adds.

"What does yours do, Ali?" Gabriella asks, and Ali snaps her head back towards us.

"Oh, um, it's hard to explain. I've only seen it once or twice. It kind of glows, like Stewart said." Gabriella raises an eyebrow and then nods. Ali looks away again.

"Why don't you both just look around a little?" Stewart asks. "See if anything jumps out."

I take a step towards an empty section.

"Ali, I really think you should just give it a try," Gabriella says. "I know you're having a hard time believing this for some reason, but someone's fate might need you to change it. And you could be missing that."

"I just don't get why . . ."

"Why what?" Gabriella asks.

"Forget it."

"No, go ahead," Stewart says, standing and facing her. "Tell us so that we can help."

She pauses and then says, "Let me just walk around with James for today."

She hurries over to my side as I walk towards a corner of the wall, and I don't stop to look back at the others.

I crouch down as Stewart had done and run my hand over the grainy cement where there is a white heart scribbled and then the initials "JR." There doesn't seem to be anything special about it.

"Tell me the truth," Ali suddenly hisses in my ear.

"Anything?" Stewart calls from across the lounge. I look over and shake my head at him and then turn back and meet her eyes.

"What?" I whisper.

"The truth." She is glaring at me now. "Can you hear them?"

"What?" I scrunch up my face. "Them?" I motion my head in Gabriella and Stewart's direction, and she narrows her eyes at me.

"No, that's not what I mean."

"I have no clue what you are talking about then."

"Nothing?" Gabriella says, suddenly leaning over us.

"Not so far," I say, but when I turn back towards the wall the name "Douglas Arsenault" glows in glittery green letters.

Margot

She hates being late, so she quickens her pace through the hallway. Freed by the last bell of the day, students are swarming in groups and then scattering out the doors. James trails behind her, watching her hair swish from side to side, expecting to follow her out one of the exits, but she turns to go up a flight of stairs. He reaches out to grab her hair without thinking about it but misses.

By the time she enters the library, her backpack slung over one shoulder and her back slightly hunched, she has slowed down.

James watches from the library entrance as she drops her bag with relief on the floor next to a table, plunks herself into a chair, and folds her arms. He notices her eyes dart back and forth from the table to the fiction section where *The Great Gatsby* sits in the same spot as yesterday on the shelf. She bites her lip and begins to tap her foot.

A few minutes later a boy walks in, blue oxford half untucked, carrying a binder that looks like it is sprouting paper. She looks up at him and gives a little wave. James instinctively raises his hand to wave back but then realizes his mistake and drops it to his side.

"Hey," the guy says as he slides the binder from his arms to the table. There is an apologetic tone to his voice. "Sorry, but . . ."

Margot waves the apology away. "It's fine, I just got here."

"Oh, yeah . . . I was actually going to say I need to do something quickly before we get started." She raises her eyebrows. "I'll just be five minutes." He holds up five fingers and smiles. The annoyed look on her face softens, and she nods.

"Yeah, sure." Her eyes remain on him as he turns and takes long strides towards the library doors. James searches her face for some sign of annoyance once the boy is gone, but it is blank. Instead, she turns her head back towards the fiction shelves.

After a moment she picks up her backpack from the floor beside her, unzips the front pocket, and roots around until her hand emerges clutching a small white piece of paper. She unfolds it on the table, smoothing it with both hands.

James moves closer until he is standing over her. She scratches her head, and he cranes his neck to see what is written on the paper. It's the number 62.

"Sixty-two," she mouths to herself. She stands and glances around with nervous eyes before hurrying over to the fiction shelves to the Fs. James follows and stands at the end of the aisle. When will seeing her not feel like a punch to the stomach? He takes in her profile.

Her index finger hooks the book off the shelf faster than she means for it to, and it topples to the ground. The green pencil that James had strategically planted rolls across the gray floor and Margot scurries to pick it up. She closes her eyes and exhales.

When she opens them, she stares straight at the end of the aisle. James pretends to meet her eyes and for a moment even entertains that she sees him. Bent down on one knee, she turns her attention to the book and begins leafing through it.

"Page sixty-two," she whispers as she clutches the pencil and flips pages, her eyes scanning from side to side. "Sixty-two."

She stops turning and begins to run her finger over a page before shifting the pencil into her right hand and drawing what seems to be a series of fast lines. She drops the pencil in the middle of the page and then slams the book shut in a hurry. She looks up as she stands, making sure she hasn't drawn any attention to herself, and then jams the book back into the open space it came from on the shelf.

She hurries back to the table. Douglas is still not back.

She crumples up the white piece of paper on which she had written the page number and rolls it around in her hands before placing it back in the pocket of her bag.

James still stands at the end of the aisle, frozen. He can't possibly risk opening the book now. He glances over his shoulder at the table where Margot sits with her chin in her hand.

It's another five minutes before Douglas comes back in, only quickening his steps once he notices Margot's eyes on him.

"I'm sorry," he starts once he reaches her. "I forgot something, and then I needed to check and see if someone turned it into the office, and . . ." The smell of cigarettes emanates from him, and he runs his fingers through his hair as he pauses, trying to figure out what to say next. She wonders for a moment why he doesn't just vape and avoid the smell.

"It's fine," she says, rising. "We probably don't have enough time to finish it all up right now. The library closes in fifteen minutes. I'll just do it myself tonight. I really don't mind." She slings her backpack over one shoulder and smiles at him. "Really." The time it will take to do it all herself will be worth it if she can just get back to her room. Take the pill she's too afraid to take before school. Be away from everyone.

Douglas stares back at her, trying to read her expression. She raises her eyebrows at him and then turns and leaves.

As soon as James sees her exit the library door, he flies down the aisle to the book. He is careful not to let the pencil fall out as his eyes scan the page, stopping on some sharp underlining.

"I felt a haunting loneliness sometimes . . ."

James

She wrote me back. I stared at it all night.

The next morning as I'm waiting inside for Margot, I notice my ribbon is still up on Kyle Morrison's locker. One afternoon I watched as he stared at it and then patted it twice before opening his lock. In a way, it was nice to see it still there. Just the other day I saw Ms. Brown pull one off her door and shake her head. I guess the time she was willing to think about me had expired.

I've been too busy keeping up with Margot to watch out for my other friends, but Kyle was solid, and I can see that he misses me, so I try to devote a little time to him. I know that he always forgets to secure his gym locker, so the other day I went in and locked it for him when he was at practice. Later that week I gave him a small push from behind so that he could come across the finish line before Jordan in their two-mile workout. Jordan's got a big head and Kyle could use some more running confidence. Kyle finished scratching his back like crazy but with a big smile on his face. Later I will have to go into Coach's office and see how the meet yesterday went, but for now, I have to get to the teachers' lounge meeting.

Ali doesn't come, so when we're done I go looking for her. She is perched against the oak tree outside the side entrance. It's her favorite spot, I'm learning, besides the orchestra room. Spanish moss hangs all around and she looks like a bird in a cage. Her legs are crossed, eyes closed.

"Hey," she says, sensing my presence as I get closer.

"Hey. Mind if I join you or are you busy?"

"No, it's fine. Have a seat." She pats the ground.

I sit down across from her and pull a blade of grass out of the ground.

"Missed you this morning."

"Yeah, just wasn't feeling it. Anything to know?"

"Not really. Teachers didn't talk about anything important. Stewart got a mission for some kid I never heard of. Freshman. Can't remember his name."

"Huh," she says. We are quiet for a minute. I watch as a lady walks her dog on the sidewalk in the distance.

"I don't hear whatever you hear," I finally say. "At least I think I don't because, to be honest, I don't really know what you're talking about." I look back from the street and meet her eyes.

She nods. "I believe you."

"What *are* you talking about though? Should I hear something?" She blinks at me and opens her mouth as if she is about to say something, but then she pauses.

"I'm not really sure, James. I'm not really sure about a lot of stuff here. I just know there's more to everything than what they let on." She motions her chin towards the school.

"What do you hear?"

She stares at me and takes a deep breath in.

"I'm not going to tell anyone."

"I hear whispers."

"Whispers?"

She nods. "It's only when I close my eyes and everything around me is quiet, but they tell me things."

"What kind of things?"

"Different things. Things that are different from what we've heard about why we are here. It's hard to explain. It might be just me." She crosses and uncrosses her legs.

"You don't believe Gabriella and Stewart then?"

"It's not that I don't believe them. I'm sure a lot of what they say is true. I just never thought that they were telling the whole story."

"So from the get-go you didn't believe what they were telling you? You're suddenly here, you're all alone with no direction. Why wouldn't you believe them?"

"Because *they* told me not to. I don't know who they get their instructions from, James, but clearly we have different sources." She shrugs and stares past me. "And in the beginning, it just didn't feel right. I mean, I didn't feel like I was supposed to be here. I guess maybe we all feel that at first, but there I was, and there they were, and I just sensed a . . . I don't know, a desperation on their part that scared me. I mean, it really scared me! It was like they wanted to attach themselves to me, and I just ran from them. Soon after I could hear the whispers, and I just knew that I didn't have to listen to Stewart and Gabriella."

"So, why are you still here then?" I ask. I swallow and look at her out of the corner of my eye, wondering if it's a question too far.

"Because they haven't told me how to leave yet. Unfortunately." The sound of a car braking screeches from the street, and we turn our heads to see an SUV just avoid hitting a delivery truck.

"I still have emotions, probably more than I should, I guess," I say.

"The emotions going away are BS, by the way. I haven't stopped being angry. I haven't stopped wanting my life back."

"You didn't numb at all?"

"Maybe a little, but it feels like work. Not something that happens naturally." She picks up a pebble and throws it close to a squirrel that has stopped to look around.

"Mine comes and goes. I'll feel sleepy, but then I wake up full of emotions."

"We all come here differently. I can't know for sure, but I think the way we cross has a lot to do with it," she says. "But I don't get why we all wouldn't numb. If we're all supposed to be doing the same thing."

"Me neither." I pause. "Stewart said it's rare, but some people never remember dying. Even after the numbing. Did you? Do you?"

"No," she shakes her head. "I went to sleep. I never woke up. And I only know that from the gossiping." She gestures with her head towards the school building again.

"So you don't feel like maybe there's a reason that we're supposed to be here?"

"Are you supposed to die from a heroin overdose at age sixteen?" she snaps.

I hesitate. "No. I mean, I don't think you're *supposed* to, but I guess bad things do happen sometimes."

"You're just accepting that mistakes never happen? That everything is as it should be?" She raises her voice, and I lean back. The squirrel is back. He stands on his hind legs and turns his head from side to side.

"I'm not accepting that. I'm just trying to figure it all out."

"The fact that we're just supposed to hover here like guardian angels, accept that our fate was the right one, well, I don't buy it. I had a life that was supposed to happen."

I take a deep breath. "But here's what I don't get. It's not like you can suddenly be alive again. It's not like Ali Townsend can suddenly rise from the dead."

"Of course not."

"So . . ."

"There are other ways to have a second chance, James. They'll just never tell you that."

"What do you mean?"

"I'm never going to get to go live the same life I had. But maybe I can go and live the type of life I was meant to have if mistakes didn't happen."

"I made a mistake," I say. She looks over at me.

"I think I forgot to look before I turned, that's all."

"That's what I mean," she says, turning her whole body to face me now. "You weren't sick! Your body didn't fail you! You didn't decide to jump off a cliff! A split-second mistake cost you your life. Don't you think there is ever the same margin for error on fate's part?"

"So why would they want to stay?"

"I haven't completely figured it out yet. The only thing I really know is that they're protecting the order of things. I'm sure they have their reasons. But I—we—don't have to agree with them."

"It's all pretty confusing," I say and look up at the sky.

"It is. Definitely."

"Yesterday, when we were looking at the graffiti, something jumped out to me."

"A mission?"

"I don't know. It was just a name. Douglas Arsenault."

She gasps and then laughs.

"You know him?"

She stares at me and narrows her eyes. "Yeah, I know him," she says, folding her arms and leaning back into the tree trunk. "We were together for a little while. He was there the night I died."

"Oh," I say. "Sorry."

"For what? I'm sorry for you. I wouldn't lift a finger for him. But he is about to need a lot of help."

"What do you mean?"

She shrugs and smiles a tiny smile. "I mean that I have stopped worrying about their rules."

"Were you worried before?"

"Not a lot. It's weird though. Something about watching them with you has made me realize I shouldn't at all. Oh, there's something else too."

"What?"

"The graffiti. I don't see it," she says, staring straight at me now.

"At all?"

"Well, I mean, I *see* it," she smiles. "It just doesn't work for me. I've never gotten a mission."

"That's weird," I say.

"Maybe. Maybe not. How would we really know anyway?"

"I see your point."

She closes her eyes again and says, "Douglas Arsenault." She laughs. "Good luck with that."

Ali holds the paper in her hand. She looks at the message again in the dim night lighting. She has never believed Gabriella and Stewart, but something makes her hesitate before she walks into Principal Logan's office to try to ruin Douglas once and for all.

It never occurred to her to really interfere with him until James got the jerk as a mission. Sure, she's thrown some of his homework away, tripped him, and made him scratch himself silly. But he doesn't deserve any help, and he doesn't deserve any saving. She shakes her head, disappointed she even entertained their warnings of not messing with the order of things. It's all BS. She knows that thanks to the whispers.

Still, she hesitates before she puts the note on top of the principal's desk. She stares down at the polished wood, the reflection of the hovering piece of paper casting a shadow over it. His face flashes into her thoughts for a moment and then she lets the paper drop.

Margot

She lay on her bed staring up at the white ceiling fan that clicks with every rotation, waiting for the pill to kick in and irritated by the conversation that she just had with her father. She asked him about the Everton enrollment deadline. Someone must have come into his office, and he started answering their questions while talking to her.

"Oh, let's not worry about that now," he said, and it didn't feel like he wanted *her* not to worry. It felt like he couldn't care less. She blinks back tears of frustration thinking of how he browbeat her to finish the application.

The tears come full force when her thoughts turn to James and how she hadn't told him. Now, like everything else, it feels like something left undone between them.

It wasn't ever that she wanted to leave James or New Orleans. He would have thought it was, though. He would have imagined it was other things when it was really that her father had insisted upon the visit to the school. And that day felt magical amongst the ivy-covered brownstones with their refinement and their air of mystery. There were offices for the literary magazine, and she could just picture herself at one of the bright white desks that lined the room. When she was there, everything inside of her suddenly felt aligned. Crooked, broken parts straightened and snapped together. It was a feeling that was undeniably right, but it was also a place without him.

"If writing is what you want, Margot, then you may as well be in the thick of it. New York is where it's at for writers," her dad said over pasta dinner at La Trattoria that night. And the fast-paced conversations, the fashionable patrons, the clinking of silverware, the glasses of wine carried by on trays, made her feel like she wanted the sleekness of it all. So she replied, "Thanks for understanding, Dad," and basked in how good it felt for him to be smiling across the table from her.

Of course, she imagined daily life without James, but it had all been on her own terms and it was fun to picture his visits. She envisioned walking through Central Park with him, even imagined the selfies in her head. There they were in the snow. There they were by the giant tree in Rockefeller Center. James would probably have done that thing where he tries to make it look like he's leaning against it or picking it up. He could never take a normal picture—except for her favorite one of them. Her head is on his shoulder and he's looking straight ahead and smiling just ever so slightly. "Best Friends," said the frame his mother had put it in. Their first kiss had been weeks before the picture, but nobody knew at the time that their relationship had turned down a different path.

Best friends. She sighs and her thoughts veer towards their last fight. James was adopted, and a few times a year his parents hosted a bunch of other adoptive families at their house. They'd been getting together and doing that for more than ten years now, and James knew a lot of the kids pretty well. She hadn't meant to put herself right in the middle of it. She had just forgotten about it and wandered down from her house figuring he wasn't paying attention to his phone. When she arrived at the kitchen door, the adults were gathered in there and James' mom insisted that she come in and join them. Moments later James came around the corner into the kitchen to grab something and the look on his face had felt like a jab to her heart.

"Hey, what are you doing here?" he said, confusion and a sprinkle of annoyance seasoning his voice.

"I forgot this was today. I just stopped by to see what you were up to. Sorry."

"You forgot?"

"I know. Stupid!" she said, shaking her head, feeling

self-conscious that the eyes of some of the adults in the room were on them.

Just then Ez came around the corner, her shiny black hair pulled to the side over one shoulder and her pouty lips slightly parted as if she were just about to say something but stopped herself when she saw Margot. Ez's parents and James' parents had been friends for a long time, and Ez had visited James' house a lot with her parents and younger brother Cam over the years. It had been a while since she'd seen her, and Margot had to admit to herself that Ez had gotten beautiful, despite the fact that she did little to conceal her sour look at Margot.

"I'm sorry for interrupting. James, just call me later or something," Margot said as she backed towards the door.

"You can stay if you want," James said.

She shook her head, waved to the group of adults picking at food on the counter, and headed out the door. Ez folded her arms and watched her leave.

Later that night as they did homework in his bedroom, Margot stretched out on his floor, propped her back up against a wall, and said, "What's up with Esmerelda these days? She looked like she wanted to spit on me earlier."

"Ez? N-n-no, she didn't." He stared at his computer screen.

"Well, I was looking right at her. She kind of did!"

"Maybe she was j-j-just surprised to see you. You know, you usually don't turn up at the Adoptive Family Support Group reunions." He peered at her over his laptop.

"I mean, I just forgot it was happening," she said softly. She looked down at her feet and wiggled her toes. "It wasn't like I was trying to crash the party."

"Yeah, I know," he said tapping on his keyboard.

"What do you guys even do at these things?" she asked, twirling the pen she was holding. "I mean, I get it when you all were little kids running around and playing, but . . ."

"What do you mean, 'What do we do?' We've b-b-been friends for years. We just catch up and stuff."

She nodded and tapped the pen on her textbook.

"And our parents are all really close, obviously. Why are

you being so w-weird about it?" he asked.

"I'm not! You guys were the ones being weird when I walked in."

They sat in silence for a moment, and Margot reread the same two sentences of her history homework that she had been fighting to move past for the last ten minutes.

"We're just a group of friends that get each other, I guess." He shrugged while he typed.

"I guess it's good to have people that get you."

"It is. Why are you s-saying it like that?"

She blinked. "It's not like you don't have other friends that get you too."

"Not like that, Margot. We don't talk about it a lot, but you c-c-can't understand what it's like to wonder about your whole existence sometimes."

But she wanted to understand. She wanted him to talk to her about it, but the disconnect felt too large. She felt her eyes starting to water, so she slammed the book shut and stood up.

"I'm going to go," she managed to squeak out.

"Are you serious right n-now?" he asked, putting his laptop down next to him. "What is even happening here?" She grabbed her things and managed to make it downstairs and out the door before the tears started.

Later that night, after she had gone out to dinner with her mother, she lay on her bed with earphones on, listening to music and staring at the ceiling. He hadn't texted her, and she was thinking about what she wanted to say to him when she heard faint knocks on her door through the music. She popped her earbuds out to ask her mother what she wanted, but the door cracked open and James' face leaned in. Her stomach did a little flip at the sight of him.

He walked over to her bed, sat down next to her, and kissed her forehead.

"I don't know what happened," he whispered. "But I don't want you to be s-sad."

"I just felt left out. And then I acted stupid . . ." she whispered back and then sniffled. She sat up and hugged him, and they had stayed like that for a while, the only sound being the muffled music still coming out of the earphones on her bed.

Her breathing feels like it is slowing down. She took an extra half today. Her stomach turned when she looked at the little brown bottle hidden in an old boot in her closet, the white sticker on the front of it peeling up at the edges, and noticed that the first batch was almost five months ago after the knee surgery. Her mom got them refilled once and another time was after she had a tooth pulled. They're going away faster now. She will have to figure something else out. Remembering the feeling of his arms around her, she closes her eyes and curls up into a fetal position.

"I should have told you that I applied," she whispers into the stillness of her room. "I'm sorry."

She is exhausted by the time biology class rolls around the next day. She slept much of the day but then was up all night, lying awake staring at the ceiling. She had been doing that thing again where she tried to sense James. She wasn't sure what it was about the stillness and the solitude of the late-night hours that made it seem like the perfect time for otherworldly things, but the privacy of it, the feeling of being utterly alone, made it seem like the ideal time to wait and hope. She reasoned that if she could sense him, she'd know the book was real too. But then morning came, as did the disappointment and exhaustion.

Before she starts towards the classroom, she double-checks her binder to make sure that she remembered to put the biology assignment in there last night. She doesn't trust herself when she is this tired.

The bell rings as she walks through the classroom door. She peers around for her lab partner but doesn't see him and just heads for the nearest open table.

Mrs. Farley sticks her head in the classroom door. "Dealing with a copier jam, people, so just sit tight."

A buzz starts to take over the room when she leaves. Kimberley is not here today, and not having anyone to talk to she opens her binder and pretends to sift around for things. The door opens again and this time it is Douglas, his eyes darting toward Mrs. Farley's desk. Margot smiles as he looks around the room. His face eases, and he begins to walk towards her.

"You got lucky," she says as he pulls out a stool. "Farley is making copies."

He smiles and runs his hands through his hair. She catches the faint scent of cigarettes.

"Why do you smoke?" she asks as he swings his backpack off his shoulder.

"What?" he says without looking at her and giving a nervous laugh.

"Cigarettes. Why do you smoke?"

His eyes widen, and he shrugs his shoulders. "Um, I don't really know, I guess. Calms the nerves." He dips his chin so that his hair falls in front of his face and he stares ahead.

"Really?"

"Yeah," he says, facing her. He shrugs again.

"I get really nervous too," she says. "Or maybe anxious is a better word."

He smiles. "Oh yeah?" His eyes turn up at the corners and seem to smile with the rest of his face.

"Yeah," replies Margot in a soft tone. "I hate it."

He nods. "Me too. Keeps me up at night."

"Oh my god, me too," Margot says. Then she lowers her voice and adds, "Did it get worse for you after . . . ?"

"After what?"

"After Ali?"

He shakes his head and looks away.

"Um, no. It's always been like that for me."

"Oh. I'm sorry. I didn't mean . . ."

He waves her off. "It's fine. I mean, I don't really like to talk about her that much, but it's fine."

Margot nods, but she has so many other questions that she wants to ask him. Like, does he ever try to sense Ali? She remembers the sight of them, entangled in the hallway, and the way they'd all watched in astonishment (and maybe with a little bit of envy too), as Ali began transforming into a girl who didn't seem to care about much anymore. It couldn't be that he'd just forgotten all about that girl with the light green eyes and the severe black eye makeup. The one that hung from his arm laughing. How could he not want to think of her much?

"Hey, thanks for doing that homework," he says.

She smiles. "It was no big deal. Just a quick summary."

Margot stares at the door, wishing Mrs. Farley would return. She yawns and stretches. Her yawn causes Douglas to yawn and they both laugh.

"I seriously have to start getting more sleep," says Margot.

Douglas looks at her. He takes in the light smattering of freckles across her nose that you probably wouldn't notice unless you were sitting this close to her. Her eyes seem puffy and slow like they are the only honest things on a pretty face. Like she is just trying to get through the day without giving anything away. But he recognizes it. Can practically smell it on her too. The telltale signs of a mind filled with what-ifs and regret and loss. Something in his chest softens.

He might have stared a few seconds too long. She catches him out of the corner of her eye and smiles as if she is questioning him.

"Maybe if you ever get caught up on your sleep, we can hang out sometime," he says.

Margot nods. "Yeah," she says, surprised at how much she means it. "That'd be great."

The classroom door opens, and Sister Ellen is there, wrapped in her yellow sweater. "Excuse me, but Douglas Arsenault is needed in the office," she says.

James

In the morning I bump into Gabriella on my way out to the stairs. "I have a mission in the lunchroom. Want to take a walk?" she asks. I don't want to. I want to go see if I can find Margot, but I never feel comfortable telling her that. Instead, I nod and just hope it will go quickly.

"What's the mission?" I say as we walk past a group of girls laughing. I pause and stuff Phillip Thomas's homework—hanging halfway out of his backpack—back in and then keep walking.

"Amy Kendall. Her name came up in the graffiti for me. Food allergy and the reaction is going to be pretty bad. Just making sure the EpiPen is where it should be." I nod.

It isn't yet lunchtime, but the cafeteria is busy. A radio blares as two of the younger food service workers walk about setting napkin dispensers down on the tables. The smell of the room is still so familiar—a mixture of rotten food and the bleach spray they use to wash the tabletops.

"Did you have a table?" Gabriella asks as we walk in.

"Usually that one," I say, pointing to one of the weathered brown vinyl bench-style tables in the far corner. "But we mostly would sit outside if the weather was good."

"They added the outdoor picnic tables after my time," Gabriella says. "But I think I would have liked them a lot. My table was usually this one." She points right in front of us a few tables to the right.

"Right there? It's pretty close to the faculty table."

Gabriella shrugs. "Yeah, I know. I wasn't exactly a rebel." She laughs and we walk over and sit. "I have to wait until they go back into the kitchen for a bit," she explains.

Around us, the young men sway and sing along with the radio as they plunk down the napkin dispensers. "Baby!" one of them wails, hitting a high note. An older skinny man with a baseball cap hurries out of the kitchen and begins putting fresh black bags into the massive garbage cans.

"I used to think this was one of those sanctuary places." She smiles, patting at her fluffy hair, which only springs back up each time. "You know, one of those places that you can grab some quiet when you need it. I was wrong!"

The two younger workers are clapping now and laughing. "Come on, Carl!" they call at him as he continues his work with the garbage cans. "Let's hear you now, baby!" Carl shakes his head at them and rolls his eyes, which only seems to fuel them on. They are both singing louder and louder.

"I think they're actually pretty good," Gabriella says, raising her voice to be heard above theirs. "I always try to think of a band name for them."

I laugh. "And does Carl ever join in?"

"Never." She shakes her head and smiles. "But that does not stop them."

Carl hurries back into the kitchen when he finishes. One of the young men actually does a backflip down the middle of the aisle. Gabriella laughs and claps.

"What happens when they run out of napkin dispensers?" I ask.

Gabriella shrugs. "They move into the kitchen and it gets kind of loud in there."

Smells of food are starting to waft around the room now. I try to decide what it is. Salisbury steak?

The guys are clapping high five and setting out the last of the dispensers at the other end of the cafeteria. A woman from the kitchen comes out with a sour look on her face and turns their radio down.

"Feels so weird to be in here like this," I say. "Familiar spots that are still familiar, but just not what they were."

Gabriella nods. "I know what you mean."

"Do you remember dying?" I ask, turning to look at her. Her blue eyes shift back and forth.

She hesitates. "Yeah, I do. I mean, I don't like to think about it all that much, but I do."

"Sorry, I didn't mean to bring up something upsetting."

"It's not upsetting. It's just strange how clearly I can still see it all. That weirds me out sometimes." She shifts around and gets a pensive look on her face. "I mean, it's insane how beautiful that day was. It was a couple of weeks after Christmas. One of those cold sunny days . . ."

I nod. "I know the type you mean."

"I had just dropped off my friend Leah. We had been at the mall. That's one thing I am really glad about. That it was just me. I think Leah had a really huge life in front of her."

"You don't think you did?" I ask.

"Well, obviously I didn't, James." She laughs.

"But . . ." I look toward the kitchen and the sounds of pots clanging and then wait for the noise to stop as one crashes to the floor and rattles around. "I mean, don't you ever kind of wonder why you and not Leah?"

"I guess I did a little at first. But then it all started to make sense."

I stare at the wall as she makes her way over to the red emergency box by the window. She feels for the key on top of it, pops it in, and opens it.

"It will for you someday, too. I promise."

"Can I ask you something?" I say, staring down at the dirty linoleum floor.

"Sure. EpiPen is here by the way. Phew."

"Does it ever make you, I don't know, *sad* to be here or anything? I mean, we're stuck here, and there's all this life going on around us, and . . ."

"No," she says, turning to look at me. "It doesn't. I feel happy that we can help them. Make their lives better somehow." Her expression is blank.

"I get that, but it's not what I really meant."

"I think I know what you mean. You mean do we get sad that we died? Does being here watching kids go on with lives we don't have anymore make us envious?"

"Well, yeah."

"Those emotions, to the extent that you even have them now, James, won't stay with you." I look up and our eyes meet. "I promise. You're where you're supposed to be. Behind the scenes here."

I think of Margot and my parents, and it's definite sadness that burbles around in the back of my throat before I swallow hard to clear it.

"Do you think they ever know we're here?"

She smiles. "Not really. And they shouldn't. That's dangerous."

"Dangerous?"

"If they were to know that we're here, it could lead to all sorts of problems."

I swallow. "So what happened with Ali?" I ask. "Like when she first got here?"

Gabriella raises her eyebrows. "It was rough. She was screaming. She was curled up in a little heap by the lockers in the science corridor. I think she must have remembered going to sleep after the, well, after she did the heroin, and when she woke up here, she must have thought she couldn't wake herself from a bad dream or something."

"Yeah," I say, remembering the same feelings from my arrival.

"I mean, she didn't tell me any of this. It's just sort of my own theory. She stood up right away when she saw me. She kept saying, 'Something's wrong, something's wrong,' and grabbing my arm. I just kept telling her that she was going to be okay. That it was all going to be okay. She kept yelling at Stewart, 'Tell Clinton something is messed up with this crap. It's bad.' We sat with her until she calmed down a little, but then she got up and ran away."

"And then what?"

"I found her in the bathroom later. She wouldn't come near me. Locked herself in a stall. I tried to explain everything I could to her. I'm not sure what she heard and what she didn't."

"That's tough."

"Have you talked with her much? I worry about her sometimes. I worry that she doesn't fully realize why she's here. And how much she's needed."

"No." I'm not sure why I lie.

"Well, anyway. Looks all good here. Why don't we go see what Stewart is up to?"

"Yeah sure," I say, standing. "Gabriella?"

"Yes?" She turns around to look at me.

I pause and then say, "How do I know that I can trust you?"

"Because you can," she answers and starts to walk away.

Margot

She taps her foot and glances from side to side, forgetting her surroundings for a moment. When she checked the book again before leaving school, there was something new in it, and the image of it—the words underlined with the deep gray of James' old pencil—keep invading her mind, taking over the landscape of her thoughts like a weed.

"All I kept thinking about, over and over, was 'You can't live forever; you can't live forever.'"

She catches herself holding her breath and then lets out a long, silent exhale. How does that happen and she doesn't even realize it? She steadies herself, suddenly recognizing that she is in a new place and it requires her attention.

She's not sure how she got here, what compelled her to say yes. All she knew was that she wanted to say no to Kimberley and Joy so badly. They were clueless about why she never wanted to go to the coffee shop after school anymore, and it was exhausting to fake feeling as if she didn't want to crawl out of her skin every time she sat with them and tried to focus on their conversations about things she no longer cared about. So instead she said yes to Douglas Arsenault.

Now he has his hand on her shoulder. It feels heavy, and her posture becomes lopsided, but she doesn't move it away. They stand underneath the open garage door of Jack Delaney's house.

In the driveway, there are two small C-shaped ramps that Jack and Casey Bennett alternate skateboarding back and forth between. The swooshing sound of the wheels is rhythmic. Two other boys she does not recognize are shooting basketballs at the other end of the driveway.

She feels the stares of the girls behind her. They unstack some plastic chairs stored in the garage and make a semi-circle out of them. When she had walked in with Douglas, Karen Anderson exhaled her cigarette, rolled her eyes, and turned to another girl Margot did not recognize, snickering something that made their shoulders shake with silent laughter. There is a deeper, earthier smell of marijuana lingering underneath the cigarette smoke, but she doesn't see anyone smoking it.

There has been a pit in the bottom of her stomach since she arrived, but there is something else there too. Some other piece of herself that felt as if it had been unplugged now feels reconnected. She can feel the spark of it inside her, like wires crossing.

"You want to go inside?" Douglas asks. She nods. They pass the girls in the garage, whose eyes flicker back and forth between each other, speaking their own secret language. In the past, she would have felt insecure, but something about it makes her want to smile. They walk through a door and into a television room.

"Hey man," says an older looking boy who peers up from the couch at Douglas. He reaches into the pocket of his tee-shirt and places something into Douglas's hands as they high five. "Hadn't forgotten about that. Figured I might see you today." He grins.

"Thanks, man," Douglas responds with a half-smile, but he shifts his weight and swallows hard.

The boy looks up at her. She feels her stomach start to clench but she smiles and then looks over at the other side of the room. "Uh, this is Margot," Douglas says, gesturing to her.

She holds up her hand and does a little wave. Immediately regretting this, she puts it down and says, "Hello."

One corner of the boy's mouth begins to smile, and he looks at Douglas before turning back to her and saying, "Good to meet you."

"This is Jack's brother. Clinton," Douglas says.

Margot nods. "Nice to meet you."

Clinton stands, clasps both hands over his head, and stretches his lanky body, exposing a toned stomach underneath his tee-shirt. Margot turns her head toward the wall.

"Y'all want the TV? I was just going to head upstairs." His eyes seem to smile at Douglas. She can feel him staring at her too, but she is careful not to meet his eyes. She is not sure why.

"Yeah, sure," says Douglas. "Thanks."

"No problem. See ya," Clinton says as he strolls out of the room.

Douglas flops down on the couch and pats the spot next to him. She hesitates and then sits down.

"What's his deal?" she asks, motioning her head toward the kitchen into which Clinton had just disappeared.

"Clinton?" Douglas shrugs. "No deal really. Did a year at LSU. I don't really know what he's doing now besides hanging around here."

Margot nods.

"He parties a lot," Douglas says after a couple moments of silence, turning to smile at her, his green eyes looking out at her from beneath strands of hair.

It is getting darker outside. The television is starting to light up the room as the sun begins to dial itself down. Margot hears the skateboards bumping on the pavement outside. It sounds like they're attempting jumps now.

"Thanks for coming," Douglas says, and she turns to look at him.

"Sure. I'm glad I did." She smiles and then looks away again, confused by the feelings that are starting to take hold.

There are empty snack wrappers on the coffee table in front of them. Behind them is a ping-pong table. In the corner, a litter box.

Jack Delaney's house. It feels so foreign, and yet something about the foreign feels so much better than the familiar. The familiar right now is filled with lonely moments during which she catches herself holding her breath, the nagging feeling of loss tapping her on the shoulder every time she forgets it for a minute.

Douglas reaches across the couch and grabs her hand. It feels good, the weight and the warmth of it are reassuring.

She doesn't realize that she is crying. It is only when his other hand reaches over and wipes a tear off her face that she notices the wetness.

"Sorry," she says shaking her head and letting out a nervous laugh. "I don't know why."

"It's fine," he says. "I get it."

They sit in silence, the sun slipping farther away outside and his hand staying on top of hers. She is usually home by now, safe in the confines of her room, but she does not want to move. She wants to stay awhile longer in the unfamiliar.

James

I open the locker and stare before picking up the uniform, rubbing the fabric together between my fingers. Every object that I encounter in the real world now feels like a soft touch, like an exhale that would barely blow out a candle, and I miss the rough feeling of the jersey that I used to complain about, especially when it needed to be washed.

Nobody's remembered my gym locker yet, or maybe they have and just don't want to deal with it, to deliver yet another sad bag of goods to my parents. I remove the uniform and slam it shut, amazed at the quiet darkness of the locker room. I have been thinking a lot about coming to a practice. Sitting down on the bench in the midst of the shouting and smack talking. Maybe at some point I will.

I'm probably not supposed to be using physical objects like this, but outside, sitting on the bottom row of the bleachers, I lace up my spikes anyway and glance around. One coach is locking up the equipment shed far off. Nothing to worry about. There's no way he can see the jersey.

Out of habit, I stretch, even though it doesn't give me the same feelings of tension being released as it once had. I just like the routine of it.

I start out at a slow pace, even though I know I won't get tired. None of it is the same. I found this out when I went running with Stewart on one of my first lonely days. But it is something—some rope that stretches from my current state into my old life—even if I can't feel my muscles working or the constant of my breathing or the sweat starting to form on my brow and the back of my neck.

It doesn't matter, though. It's the remembering that I want. The way the trees look when you round the first bend. The way you can hear the street noise in the background.

Crunch, crunch, crunch. I let my feet hit the ground, smile at the marks my spikes leave. Their dots form a trail of proof behind me that this is really happening. That I am here.

I checked the book before I decided to run. She must have replied while I was in the teachers' lounge this morning, watching Ali repeatedly hit the cancel button on the copy machine every time a teacher came in to use it.

"People disappeared, reappeared, made plans to go somewhere, and then lost each other, searched for each other, found each other a few feet away."

A wave of emotion starts to form. Sadness, I think; I can't really tell for sure. I felt it in the library, staring at the page, remembering how sometimes we would just stare at each other, the first one to look away loses. I start to kick harder.

"What are you doing?" I hear Gabriella's voice cry out. Her tone is a mixture of amusement and admonishment.

"Running," I answer, starting to go even faster.

"You're lucky none of them wanted to stick around today," she calls.

"That's why I am doing it!" I yell, rounding a bend and leaving her staring at my back.

I feel her eyes on me as she folds her arms and stands there, the early evening sky starting to turn orange while the outside lights on timers begin to spring on.

The next day I run with Stewart. "I'm glad to have someone to do this with," Stewart says as we start to jog our second lap around the school grounds.

"Yeah, thanks for inviting me," I say. "Feels good." I look out at the street as we circle by, wishing that I could sprint into it, leave these grounds, and see the world again.

"It's funny," Stewart calls over his shoulder as he pulls slightly ahead of me, his head of curls bobbing. "It has the same effect for me as when I was alive. Clears my head."

I wish it would clear my head too, but it's swirling with all of the things I usually sit and think about on the bleachers. Still, something about it feels good and normal.

"Stewart?" I say, straining to be heard over his sudden humming.

"Yep?"

"How do you know when you get a mission? And if you do, what are you supposed to do?"

"Do you think that you got one?"

"Well, I don't really know. I might have."

He slows his pace so that we are running side by side again. "If you think that you did then you probably did," he says.

I shrug and roll my eyes a little.

"Don't be overwhelmed," he says. "But you should really start shadowing the person."

"I didn't know him."

"Well, if that's the case we can look him up in the yearbook and then find his locker assignment or schedule in the office so you can know where to find him. Who do you think you got a mission for?"

"Douglas Arsenault," I say. He nods. "You know him?"

"I know who he is, yeah. I can see why he might need a little watching." He glances sideways at me and smirks.

"Well, if he needs something important maybe you or Gabriella should take this one."

"Can't," he says, pulling ahead again. "Doesn't work that way. Has to be the person that it got assigned to."

"I have no idea what I am supposed to do for him though."

"The graffiti didn't tell you?" He scrunches up his face.

"No, it just highlighted his name for me."

"That's strange," he says. "So yeah, you have to find him then. Shadow him and it should become pretty clear how you can help him."

I don't want to shadow Douglas Arsenault, whoever he is, and I don't want to be running with Stewart anymore. I want to be by myself and go find Margot and then check the book.

Margot

She's only here because Hailey's mom called her mother and personally invited Margot to the birthday dinner. It was easier to go than to explain all the reasons why she didn't want to.

Hailey's mom has been making birthday pasta dinners since they were little and it has become a weird tradition that's carried over to their teen years. Now Margot sits in the bricked patio of Hailey's backyard, which is draped with streamers and twinkling white lights, listening to the laughter that is just slightly louder than the already loud music. It all just feels like noise, and she shifts in her seat.

Kimberley's laugh is the loudest and she turns to Margot with a forkful of salad in her hand and says, "It's so true! I mean, did you see her?"

Margot blinks. "Um, what? I'm sorry, I didn't hear who you were talking about."

"Jennifer Ayles," Tessa says from across the table before taking a sip from the childlike rainbow "Happy Birthday" cup in front of her.

"Oh. I haven't seen her lately," Margot says and moves a piece of lasagna from one side of her plate to the other.

"Well, you're missing out. She's got a weird new goth thing going on."

Margot forces a smile and shrugs. Elenore is making some sort of comment about black lipstick that she can barely hear.

Kimberley came over to get ready for the party with her. It all felt staged, this night of companionship, clearly coordinated without her input. But as Kimberley was putting on mascara in front of the full-length mirror in Margot's bedroom the same way she always did when they prepared to go somewhere together, the familiarity of the sight made her want to confide in her about the book.

"Kim?" she had asked.

"Uh-huh?" Kimberley responded without turning around and continued to pile on the mascara.

"I know this is going to sound weird, but . . ."

Her mother knocked on the door.

"Are we ready, ladies?" she asked in an overly cheerful voice. Margot nodded.

"Be downstairs in a minute, Mom."

"What's going to sound weird?" Kimberley asked.

Margot hesitated. "Nothing. Just that I was thinking about changing. I feel overdressed."

"That *is* weird! You look great!"

She's glad now that she didn't share her secret as she looks at the carefree faces around the table and pictures it being the subject of a group discussion about how strange she's gotten.

Hailey's mom bursts through the French doors with a large sheet cake singing "Happy Birthday" and everyone joins in. Margot looks at her phone underneath the table.

"What are you up to," she texts to Douglas.

"Who are you texting?" Kimberley whispers as Haley blows out the candles.

"Oh, I was just responding to Douglas."

"Ugh, *why?*"

Margot shrugs. "He's just a friend," she says in a tiny voice as the other girls clap and then talk over each other as the cake is being cut.

"Since when? I don't get it, Margot," she says, shaking her head and rolling her eyes. "And he's probably about to be expelled anyway after someone left that note in the principal's office."

"What note?"

"The one that said he was with Ali Townsend the night she died. I heard they're reopening the investigation." Margot's stomach dips as Haley's mom places a piece of cake in front of her.

She waits for him to tell her about it, but he doesn't. It was probably some ridiculous rumor that Kimberley and the rest of her friends ran with. Whatever, she doesn't need them now.

She's been coming to Jack's house with Douglas for weeks at this point and the girls still have not softened. They are not mean to her, they don't snicker as much under their breath, but they don't talk to her either. She doesn't care though. Maybe it's the antidepressants her mother put her on, maybe it's the fact that she doesn't have enough care left in her to give them any, but she barely notices them anymore. Her own friends have stopped waiting for her between classes, stopped inviting her out on the weekends.

This Friday afternoon is busier than usual. Jack's dad is out of town, leaving Clinton in charge. Her insomnia is worse than ever, but she has a strange energy despite the lack of sleep. Douglas says it's probably the antidepressants. She has never told him about the other pills. She's taking them almost every day now. She keeps telling herself she'll stop. She just needs to figure everything out a little more. There's music blaring and her body is feeding off the noise and vibration of it.

On the way here her thoughts were consumed by the book. It's always hard to leave it for the weekend, and she'd barely found the time to run back up to the library before meeting Douglas. The quote that was waiting for her is ping-ponging around her head.

"He talked a lot about the past and I gathered that he wanted to recover something, some idea of himself perhaps, that had gone into loving Daisy."

Lately, sometimes even when she concentrates really hard, she has to fight for the details. The slight flush in his cheeks that seemed to always be there no matter the temperature, the way he'd always rock back and forth a little bit when he hugged her. It can't really be James, though. It's just someone else who loves the book too. They're playing a game, them and her. It's just for fun. But the pencil. She always comes back to the pencil.

A flash of his crumpled car suddenly pops into her mind's eye, and she shakes her head to get rid of it. A boy she doesn't recognize whizzes by her on a skateboard, and she realizes that Douglas is tapping her on the shoulder.

"Want something to drink?" he asks.

"Sure." Does she? She chases away any responsible thoughts and sticks with her answer, which makes her smile. No more overthinking. She watches the skateboarding boys as Douglas disappears into the crowd and then returns with two red plastic cups.

"Vodka and Sprite," he says and shrugs.

"Thanks."

He raises his cup at her. "Here's to the weekend," he says and takes a sip.

"Seriously," she agrees and does the same.

"So are you good with hanging here awhile?"

"Yeah," she says, swallowing hard because soda always makes her need to burp. "I'm totally fine with it. Why? Did you want to go somewhere else?"

He shrugs. "We can just play it by ear. I'm good for now."

"Hey man," says Clinton, who walks up behind Douglas and pats his shoulder then comes around the front and extends his hand.

"Hey, Clinton, what's up?" says Douglas as his posture stiffens.

"Not much, not much. Just about to order some pizza if y'all want some. Just collecting a few bucks if you do."

"You hungry?" Douglas asks, turning to Margot. Clinton looks over at her as if he's just noticed her presence. He raises his eyebrows and smiles.

"Um, no. No, I'm good," she says and takes another sip of her drink.

"Yeah, me too," Douglas agrees, turning back to Clinton.

"Thanks though."

"Alright. Just don't like to see people go hungry!" Clinton's laugh is forced.

Douglas nods and smiles before looking down at his sneakers.

"See me later though, okay? I may have something you like." Clinton winks at him and then nods at Margot before walking away.

She takes a gulp of her drink. It tastes more like vodka than it does like Sprite, but it feels like a challenge now to deal with its unpleasantness since it has already started to make her feel a little warm, like there is the promise of numbing her body more than she already has been.

"You don't like him much, do you?" she asks, sloshing the drink around in the cup. A gnat has found its way in and she fishes it out with her pinky.

"What? Why do you say that?" Douglas laughs and runs his fingers through his hair. It has become his go-to response to her annoying habit of asking direct questions.

She shrugs. "Just seems like you don't."

"I've known Clinton for years," he says, staring straight ahead at the skateboarders.

"Doesn't mean you like him." Margot smiles.

"It's complicated."

"How so?"

"Jesus!" he says, shooting her a sideways look and taking a sip of his drink. "Just is."

"Sorry . . ."

"No, it's fine." His tone lightens. "I'll tell you about it sometime. Just don't feel like it right now."

Margot shifts from side to side. She loves how loose her body feels, but she is also starting to feel lightheaded. "Mind if we sit down?" she asks.

"Uh, sure. You okay? Want to go inside?"

"No, right here is fine," she says, carefully lowering herself to the ground. "I just felt a little bit light-headed."

He sits down beside her, stretching his legs out and leaning back on his arms. After a couple of minutes, he roots around in his shorts pockets and pulls out a pack of cigarettes. Margot watches his expert flick of the lighter and the way he tilts his head back when he first inhales. She wonders how long it has taken him to perfect that and why he ever felt the need to.

"So what are you doing this weekend?" he asks.

"Avoiding my mother as much as possible," she says with a sigh. Douglas smiles.

"That bad?"

She pauses. "I don't know how to describe it. She means well. But it feels exhausting."

She raises the red cup to her mouth and takes a tiny sip this time. She is becoming aware of the alcohol's effect on her now.

"What are you up to?" she asks after a few minutes of silence.

"Nothing," he says. "I'll definitely give you a call."

She feels sparks of happiness flutter around inside her. They remind her of James, and she shakes her head then raises the red cup and takes another sip.

James

I name the residual that runs around the track Nick because his running form reminds me of Nicholas Johnson on my track team. It's hard to tell what year "Nick" attended St. Xavier, but Gabriella says that according to a picture and trophy in one of the glass cases in the office, he was coached by Coach Parker in the 1950s. He does have the neat, short, slicked-back hair that seems like it would have been popular during that time period. There are others that appear from time to time too, but I didn't name them. A couple of football players. Another coach.

I name Nick because I've started to enjoy the short bursts of running with him in the morning. I don't bother with the spikes and the uniform; it's just a few minutes to myself every day before I go to the library to check the book. I love going through the routine of stretching as Coach Parker paces and barks at Nick without making a sound. Then I line up next to him on the track and focus.

And Nick is fast. A sprinter. 400 meters. I like to glance over at the murky image of him when we line up. His pale eyes have laser beam focus.

"Good luck," I say, even though it's always unacknowledged. And then we're off. I've almost beaten him twice.

This rainy morning it is hard to see the faint figures of Nick and Coach Parker against the gray background of the sky. Nick's focus when he lines up is unchanged. He takes his stance. Coach Parker wrings his hands as he always does and then lifts his arm into the air and lowers it quickly to signal the start.

We are off. I'm enjoying the sound of the wind when Nick falls, just collapses onto the track about twenty feet from the finish line.

I slow my pace and stare over my shoulder as the residual clutches at his leg and Coach Parker takes off in a jog towards him. When I stop to turn around and head back towards them, they are gone.

I freeze and stare at the place where they had been, trying to make sense of what I've just seen. I've never seen them do anything but the exact same thing day after day, and something about it doesn't feel right. I can't shake the look of agony on Nick's face.

I put my hands on my hips and exhale, watch the rain add to the puddles. Then I force myself to continue running. I want to get to the library before the school opens.

When I get there the sun is blazing through the big picture window behind the circulation desk, brightening the place even though all the lights are still off. I grab the book off the shelf, sit down in the aisle, and open it.

"It was one of those rare smiles with a quality of reassurance in it, that you may come across four or five times in your life."

When I am done in the library, I decide I need to find Douglas Arsenault and watch him. I don't want to, but part of me is really curious about why he might need me, why his name lit up like that. Last night Stewart went into the office and got a yearbook and showed him to me. I didn't really recognize him, but now, as I make my way towards his locker, C204, he is there and I know him immediately as the guy Margot met in the library.

I get close up next to him as he is messing around with things in his locker, and I watch as he stuffs a weathered-looking pack of cigarettes into the front pocket of his backpack and sighs. He looks at the schedule he has taped to the inside of his locker, runs his fingers over it, and squints.

"Okay, math," he mumbles to himself. He grabs a textbook and slams the locker shut.

As he starts to walk down the hallway, he keeps his head down, not acknowledging any of the people that pass him. The back of his white uniform has mud splatters on it, and I stare at them, imagining all the ways that could have happened. He fumbles around in his pocket and pulls out a piece of gum.

"Douglas!" a voice is calling from behind us. His shoulders stiffen, but he does not stop. "Douglas!" the voice yells again. We turn at the same time and see Mr. Firenze, the assistant principal, jogging toward him.

"Listen," he says, sounding winded when he gets there, "you know you're supposed to check in with me once a week."

"Yeah," says Douglas, a combination of fear and annoyance in his eyes.

"It's Thursday and I haven't heard from you at all, Douglas."

"I was going to come see you tomorrow."

"I'm not going to be in tomorrow, Douglas," he says, raising his eyebrows. "And you would have known that if you had emailed me at the beginning of the week to set up an appointment like you're supposed to."

"I'm sorry. Can this count?" he asks and smiles.

Mr. Firenze sighs and tilts his head sideways at him. "No, it cannot count and you know that. And this is not a joke, Douglas. This is a condition of you remaining at this school."

He nods.

"I went to bat for you," he says, pointing a finger as Douglas looks at the ground. "I went to bat for you because . . ." he looks over his shoulder to make sure there is nobody else around, "because I did not believe you were ultimately at fault for the tragedy, and your dad and I go way back. But I'm going to tell you something, Douglas. I am in the minority in that belief, and you are not making it easy for me to help you. It's just a check-in, Douglas. It's not much."

"I just forgot," he says and looks up.

"Well, this will be the last time I am reminding you. Can you come in right after school?"

Later, after I watch Margot leave, I head to Mr. Firenze's office. Douglas is already there.

"What does that mean?" he is asking Mr. Firenze as I enter through the closed door.

"It means exactly what I just said. That a couple of your teachers think you're despondent. Or are you asking what despondent means?"

He nods.

"It means you seem down. Like you've stopped trying or caring."

"I'm here," he says with a shrug. "But it's kind of hard sometimes."

"What's hard? Your classes are hard?"

"No, I mean just being here. Everyone thinks I did something that I didn't do. The teachers all hate me."

"They do not all hate you, Douglas. They see a young man who needs to get his life on track." He leans forward in his chair. "Use this opportunity, Douglas. Use it! You do not want to be looking for a new high school to go to in the middle of your junior year. Finish your education here and use it to get yourself to somewhere different for a fresh start, but you've got to do your part."

"Okay," he whispers and puts his hands in his pockets.

"And then, there's the note," he sighs. "I know Principal Logan spoke with you about the note left on his desk."

"It's not true though," Douglas says, looking up. His eyes are welling.

"What's not true?"

"Yes, she was my girlfriend. Yes, I saw her that night. But I didn't give her anything, and I didn't sit there and watch her die!"

Mr. Firenze stares at him for a minute before looking down at the ground. "I believe that," he says, softening his tone. "I believe that, Douglas. And I hope the police will not feel the need to reinvestigate and make everyone relive that tragedy. Now, that being said, don't miss setting up an appointment on Monday."

He nods and stands.

"Mrs. Burns is always available to talk too."

"I'm okay. Thanks," he says, running his fingers through his hair and then turning to leave. When he's gone, Mr. Firenze closes his eyes and shakes his head. I have no idea what I am supposed to do for this kid.

Margot

She sits at the table in the library massaging her temples. She saw a porcelain turkey on Sister Ellen's desk this morning, and it was a reminder of how much time has passed. James sits down in the seat across from her and stares at her bowed head as if they are going to have a conversation.

He can't see her face, but her hands are pale and purplish. A sharp cough sounds from behind them somewhere, and she raises her head. He sighs. Her lips are dry, and underneath her eyes is darkness.

She exhales and leans over to pull something out of her backpack.

"Margot?" a voice says in an elevated whisper.

They both glance around until they see the source. Mrs. Burns. She strides towards Margot, waving, in a pants suit that looks like it was forgotten at the bottom of a closet. Margot exhales again and stares at the ceiling.

When the counselor reaches the table, she pulls out the chair next to Margot and faces her.

"I thought I might find you here. We were supposed to meet this study hall period, remember?"

"I know, but I don't really have anything I need to discuss. It's been a good week. Plus, I have some work to do."

"Well, I have to admit, I was glad to find you in the library." She raises her eyebrows at Margot, who turns and stares at the table. "But I do have some things I wanted to discuss with you."

"Like what?" Margot asks, looking up from the table.

"I'm not sure this is really the best place for a discussion." She twists her head from side to side, surveying the area.

"Is this about my French test? I swear, my mother needs to relax."

"It's not just about your French test, Margot. What do you have to work on right now? I don't see any books."

"I just have some things I need to get done for last period."

Mrs. Burns rests her elbow on the table and meets Margot's eyes. "Then when can we meet? Want to take a few minutes after school? Tomorrow's study hall?"

"I can't after school. I have to be somewhere."

"Tomorrow then?"

"Yeah, okay." Margot shrugs.

"Great," Mrs. Burns answers, pushing out the wrinkles on her pants before standing. "I will see you then." She smiles and pats Margot's back before leaving.

Margot lets out a small groan as she walks away and mumbles something that James cannot quite make out. Then she pulls out a textbook and drops it on the table. When she looks up again a smile spreads across her face, and she holds up a hand.

Douglas is looking in through one of the glass walls that separate the library from the school hallway. She signals for him to come, and he nods.

James crosses his arms and leans back in his chair. He watches her expression perk up as Douglas comes in and then has to jump out of the chair at the last minute so as not to be sat on.

"I was wondering where you were," Douglas says, smiling at her.

"Yeah, I was supposed to meet with Burns. I just wasn't up to it." She shrugs.

"Burns? Really?" He wrinkles up his face.

"Yeah. She set up this check-in time thing a while back. I didn't realize I *had* to go. But she came and tracked me down, so . . ."

"Really?" he giggles. James leans down and stares at his face. His eyes are glassy. And why is he here tracking down Margot?

"Yeah," Margot responds with a roll of her eyes. "I mean,

she's a nice lady and everything, but I think this is just about my mom freaking out about my French grade. I mean, calm down everyone, it's a bad test grade."

Douglas smiles and nods.

"Plus, I hate the way she makes me dwell on stuff, you know?"

"Dwell?"

"Well, not dwell so much, just relive things . . . I don't know! Think about things I don't feel like thinking about. I mean, I'm sure you had to meet with her when Ali—"

"Nope. Not once."

"Really?"

"Really. I was barely allowed back at school, though." Margot nods.

"Are y'all going to Jack's after school?"

"Maybe. Feel like doing something?"

"Yeah. I'm too annoyed to get to any of this work, and I'm dragging."

"Aww, wittle Margot is tired," he says, reaching across the table and patting her head. She smiles back at him, and James looks away. "We can always just go to my house."

"Okay. Yeah, that might be good. I just need some time before dealing with my mom. I'm so mad that she gets Mrs. Burns on me for one bad grade."

"I've got to go grab my stuff from my locker before world history. Want to head that way?"

"No." Margot shakes her head. "I just need to finish something up quickly. I'll meet you there after last period."

"Okay. See ya."

She watches him go and then retrieves *Gatsby*. It's not her turn to respond, but she brings it back to her table and flips through it. James stands behind her, watching as her shaky fingers leaf through the pages. She has the pencil out on the table, and she hesitates before running two fingers over it, pausing over the grooves of the teeth marks.

Then she picks it up, flips through it for a few minutes, and underlines a sentence. *"My own rule is to let everything alone."*

James

"Stop. What are you thinking right at this moment?" she asks me. Her eyes are green with flecks of yellow and brown in them. She's staring at me, waiting. It's a game we play. I love it, and I hate it. Love that she wonders what is going on in my mind, hate having to answer. Sometimes I try to come up with something out of the ordinary to respond with like, "I was wondering why penguins can't fly," but most of the time it's something more along the lines of "I was thinking about dinner."

It doesn't happen often, but this time when she asks I happen to be wondering what my birth parents are doing at this very moment. I really don't think of them much, to be honest. I was looking down at my feet, thinking about how sore they were and wondering if either of my birth parents were runners. "Thinking about you, of course," I answer casually and then stretch my arms over my head and yawn.

"Thanks for lying," she says with a smile and closes her textbook. She gets up from the floor and sits next to me on my bed, causing my dog Bear, who is sitting at the edge of it, to sigh. When she leans into me, I put my arm around her and soak her in. The weight of her head on my shoulder, the coolness of her skin.

"I do actually think of you a l-lot, though," I say, kissing the top of her forehead.

She laughs and then suddenly I am wide awake on the bleachers. I bolt upright and Ali is staring at me, her hands on my feet. For a second it still feels like the weight of Bear, and I glance down to double-check and then try to calm myself.

"I didn't mean to startle you. You were yelling, well, sort of crying out. I heard you from the tree over there. I just wanted to make sure you were okay."

"A dream," I say, swallowing. Suddenly I want it all back. The feel of

Margot next to me, the smell of her, the sound of her laugh. Loneliness feels like it's boring a hole through me, and I wrap my arms around myself.

Ali stares at me.

"I'm sorry," she says, patting my feet. "You going to be okay?"

"I miss her," I whisper. "It feels like I should still be with her. Why doesn't that numb?"

She looks back at me with sad eyes. "I don't know the answer to that."

I exhale and look up at the nighttime sky.

"I just know that for you and I something about this doesn't feel right."

I nod. "Maybe I am supposed to be someone's hero," I finally say. "But I don't know how I am supposed to do that when I spend so much of my time missing—"

"I am going to leave," she says, cutting me off.

"Yeah okay. I'm sorry, you don't have to stay. I'll be fine."

"That's not what I mean. Here. Well, *this*. I'm going back, James."

I stare at her.

"Maybe you should come too," she says softly.

"What does that even mean, Ali? You can't go back and just be you again."

"Of course not, but I can be living. And not here doing *this*."

I turn my head and stare at the school. One of the security lights flickers a little.

"Think about it," she says and stands up. "I won't be staying much longer, James. And I can help you go back too."

"I don't know," I say, looking down.

"Don't tell them, okay? I don't need endless lectures about my fate."

"Yeah, of course. I wouldn't do that."

"Soon, James," she says gliding down the bleachers and looking back at me. "I'll have all the directions soon and once I do, I'm gone."

I nod.

"Feel better," she says and waves.

I sit for a few minutes waiting for the loneliness and sadness to ease. When I recognize the numbing starting to round out the sharp edges of it all, I stand.

"Too little, too late," I mumble. I don't know what to do with myself, but I know that I need to move around.

In the library, in the faint light right before night is deciding to turn to morning, I sit in the aisle and I run my fingers over the grainy pages of the book. Finally, I underline, *"'Can't repeat the past?' he cried incredulously. 'Why of course you can!' He looked around him wildly, as if the past were here lurking here in the shadow of his house, just out of reach of his hand."*

I try to imagine what is next after here. Whatever moving on looks like, it's got to be better than looking at the painted cinderblock hallways of St. Xavier every day. It's why I'm standing outside of Mrs. Farley's biology classroom waiting for Douglas.

When I look through the little window in the classroom door, I see him staring at her. Margot doesn't know it, but as she is looking at the board and writing down notes, he is fixed on the profile of her face. Her eyes dart from the board to her paper. Her head tilts to the side when she writes and his tilts with it. I fold my arms and look away.

I wish the graffiti told me what I am supposed to do for this kid besides watch him follow Margot around. It would also be nice if it could tell me why she doesn't seem to mind. Why she'll seek him out but head in the other direction when she sees actual friends like Kimberley coming. But I don't get to know what's going on in her mind anymore. I can't believe I miss her talking at me as much as I do.

The door flies open next to me. Margot is the third one out of the classroom. Her hair is in a ponytail and it sways behind her. I want to follow her to her locker. Stand next to her even just for the few minutes that she'll take to drop some things off, run a brush through her hair, take a sip from the pale blue metal water bottle she fills every morning before first period. But I wait for Douglas instead.

When he comes out the door, he takes his phone out of his pocket, gives it a quick glance, and shoves it back in. Afterwards he looks around the hallway to make sure nobody is about to bust him for breaking the no phones during school hours policy. He waits for a moment behind a group that has stopped to talk but then sidesteps them when he realizes that they are not going anywhere. I start to follow him.

He doesn't talk to anyone as he passes people in the hallway and nobody talks to him. In fact, most of the time he is looking down at his feet. I wonder who his friends are. I think about asking Ali, but I don't want to set her off. Start her down a path of telling me about that night again.

When he stops at his locker, he pauses. I get the feeling that he spends his days just going through the motions. He starts to spin the black dial on the lock, and I scan the area as he does. Football team guys in their jerseys laugh and shove each other back and forth at the other end of the hall. Catherine Williams walks up to the locker next to Douglas and then takes a step back and folds her arms, an annoyed look on her face.

"Oh, sorry," Douglas says, clicking the lock open and looking up at her.

"It's fine, I'll wait," she replies, staring beyond him.

He starts to move faster under the pressure of her presence. Slipping the backpack off his back, he takes one textbook out to put in his locker and then reaches for another. As he does, a piece of black construction paper falls out onto the little space of floor between them.

Letters that look like they were cut from magazine advertisements are glued across it to form words. "WHY DID YOU LEAVE HER?"

Catherine's mouth hangs open at first, but she closes it as she moves her eyes from the paper to his face and glares.

I hear Douglas exhale. He bends down and grabs it, crumples it in one hand.

"Can you move now?" Catherine asks. Her tone is forceful and sounds more like a demand than a request.

"Yeah," Douglas replies and turns to close his locker. She moves into the space as he steps away, and I hear him mutter to himself, "Why does this keep happening?"

Margot

Delores Burns stacks the papers on her desk into a neat pile. She sorts through them again, reading the teachers' comments and trying to commit them to memory. She wants to be as specific as possible without having to refer to them during the meeting. She will have to handle this one carefully.

There is a soft, tentative knock on her door. She shuffles the papers again and puts a file folder on top of them before responding to it.

"Come in," she calls.

Margot's face pokes through the doorway. "I wasn't sure if you were busy," she says. Her voice is raspy. She clears her throat.

"Nope. Have this time all set aside for you." She smiles. "Come on in."

Margot's shoulders sink as she walks in and sits in the olive-colored pleather chair across from Mrs. Burns.

"So," she says, folding her arms. "What did you want to talk about?"

"How've you been doing, Margot?" Mrs. Burns continues to smile.

Margot shrugs. "The same as I have been. Things kind of suck, but I'm getting through it."

"What sucks?"

"What do you mean?" Margot looks dumbfounded.

"I mean, besides the obvious grief you still feel."

Margot shrugs again.

"Is there anything at school that's bothering you?" Mrs. Burns prods.

"Other than just being here?" They both smile and are quiet for a moment.

"How are classes going?"

"That's what this is really about, isn't it? My mom was upset about my French grade. So I bombed a test. It happens sometimes."

"It does. But not usually to you." She folds her hands and puts them on her lap. "But no, your mom did not ask me to touch base with you about your French test. I'm actually hearing a little bit of teacher concern. That's why I wanted to make sure we met."

Margot shakes her head in disbelief and stares at the ceiling. "Concern about what?"

"Concern that maybe you're getting a little off track from your studies."

"And what if I am? They don't think that may be just slightly normal considering?"

"Of course they do." Mrs. Burns tries to keep her voice even-keeled and reassuring. "Everyone just wants to help you stay on track as much as possible. College admissions are very competitive, and—"

"I don't care," Margot says, leaning back in her chair. "I don't care about college right now."

"That's the point, Margot. Right now you don't care, but what if next year you really do?"

"Then," she pauses and shrugs. "Then I'll just deal with it."

"Fair enough. But I wouldn't feel right about things if I didn't talk to you about it now instead of a year from now."

"Is there more?"

"Pardon?" Mrs. Burns straightens her posture and stares at her.

"Was that all that you wanted to talk about, or is there more?"

The counselor's thoughts shift immediately to the Arsenault boy, though she suspects that is not a topic she could touch on right now.

"Well, nothing specific, Margot. It's just that we understand that grief is not a fleeting emotion. And the school wants to continue supporting you in your time here as a student."

"So, nothing then?"

Mrs. Burns crosses her legs and stares at Margot. It's not like her to be so snide. Defensive when she is upset, yes, but something seems different. She tilts her head.

"You look tired, Margot."

"I hate when people say that." She rolls her eyes.

"Are you getting enough sleep?"

"Sometimes."

"Well, are you having difficulty sleeping?"

"Sometimes."

"Your mom told me about the antidepressants. Are they helping?"

"I guess. It's hard to tell." Margot's eyes glance up at the clock.

"Okay. I'd like to keep this weekly appointment, so please try to do your best to remember to stop in."

Margot just stares in response.

Mrs. Burns leans in. "I wouldn't request it if I didn't think it was important."

"So it's a request?" Margot raises her eyebrows.

"For now, it is."

Margot stands. "I need to get to the library quickly before next period."

"That's fine. Thank you for remembering to stop in. I'm glad I got a chance to see how you are doing."

"Bye," she says in an exasperated tone and waves before darting out the door.

Ali stands by the water fountain next to the first-floor staircase when the girl with the red hair, James' girlfriend, comes flying out of the main office. Margot, isn't it? She is busy jamming a small wad of paper towel into the water dispenser in hopes that it will spray April Taylor on her way out of the bathroom. She can't stand that girl. She was one of the more vocal "She deserved it" types at her memorial service.

Margot smashes a closed fist on the locker and looks all around, taking short, angry breaths. The girl stares at the ceiling, runs a hand through her hair, and then starts up the staircase. Ali follows.

She is moving fast. Ali has to really pay attention to keep up with her. She is surprised when she finds her making a beeline for the library.

Ali is about to abandon the plan, but then she sees James sitting at one of the tables in the back of the library, shoulders hunched.

He perks right up, though, when Margot goes to the exact table he's at and sits down across from him. "How did he know?" she wonders. It almost looks like they're about to have a conversation.

Margot checks her watch and then leaves her things on the table and wanders over to some shelves. She runs her fingers over the spines of the books as James rises, watching her every move.

Ali moves in closer but is careful to stay out of James' sight.

Margot opens a book carefully, holding it so that the pencil stuck in between the pages will not fall out. She thumbs to where the pencil is placed and looks down to read the page. Ali watches as the girl closes her eyes and turns her face up toward the ceiling. She looks like she is fighting back tears.

James moves closer, even puts his hand on her shoulder, removing it quickly when she starts to scratch at it.

"Oh, James," Ali whispers and shakes her head. Maybe she is not the only one breaking the rules.

But before she can give it much more thought, she sees Douglas come into the library. She cringes. He moves toward the table that has Margot's backpack on it and pauses there, scanning the room.

Margot starts walking back towards the table, blotchy eyed and clutching the book to her chest. Ali strains to see the title, but Margot's arms are across the front cover.

Douglas smiles when he sees her. Margot hasn't noticed him yet, but Ali watches as he waits for her to see him standing there. She remembers so well that rumpled look of his. The right hand constantly brushing his thick brown hair to the side. It always seemed too long, even after he had just had it cut, but she had liked it.

"Oh hey," Margot says, catching sight of him, and Ali thinks she detects a hint of happiness.

"So, I've decided whenever I can't find you, I just go right to the library."

"Yeah," Margot shrugs. "Nobody bothers me here."

He smiles at her. Ali recognizes that smile, and for a moment she thinks she might even feel a pang of jealousy. She closes her eyes and shakes her head.

"You want to chill out at Jack's after school? I figured after your meeting with Burns you might need it. Did you even go?"

"Yeah, I went. Pretty much what I figured, but I have to keep going every week. Whatever! At least I didn't have to stay the whole period." Ali watches as James starts to edge closer, his arms folded. "Um, let me just put this book back, and I'll walk downstairs with you."

"Okay."

Margot's arm falls slightly and Ali notices the title of the book, *The Great Gatsby*. She remembers it from freshman English class. Hated it.

Margot hurries over to the shelf where James is standing, his face riddled with disappointment, and stuffs the book in. Then she scoops up the rest of her things from the table and leaves with Douglas.

James

I'm not feeling it at all, but I decide to try. I rip out the yearbook page with Mr. Firenze's faculty picture and circle his face in Sharpie. I push the sheet through the crack in the side of Douglas's locker.

"Make your damn appointment or whatever," I grumble. Then I hear a girl screaming. I fly around the corner and see her lying on her back, her leg bent underneath her. A pool of water surrounds her and her black hair fans out around her in wet clumps.

Mr. Dempsey, one of the chemistry teachers, peers out the window of his classroom door with an angry expression until he sees her on the floor and comes racing down the hallway.

Her skirt has twisted up from the fall, and I yank it down so that her underwear isn't showing anymore. She stops screaming and is just sobbing now that there is the sound of multiple footsteps running towards her.

I look to my right. The water fountain is overflowing. One residual is standing there with his finger on the button while the other splashes water onto the floor.

Mr. Dempsey is almost to the girl, but before he can reach her he slips, breaking his fall with his right arm.

"Jesus!" he says, standing up and rubbing it as he looks down at the girl. "There's water everywhere in here!" He shoots an angry look over at the water fountain and then leans down to talk to her.

"Okay, sweetheart, is it just your leg that hurts?"

"Yes!" the girl wails.

"Did you hit your head too?"

"I . . . don't . . . know!" she says in between huge, messy sobs.

Mrs. Garcia has come out of her classroom and is making her way towards them, but she seems to have noticed the water and is taking very deliberate steps.

"Can you call for the nurse?" Mr. Dempsey asks, looking up at her, still rubbing his arm.

She nods and heads back towards her classroom. A small group has gathered now.

Stewart appears and rushes around them to where I'm standing. He looks down at the girl and frowns. I point towards the residuals and the water fountain.

"What are they doing?" Stewart asks, staring at them with a confused look.

"Everybody back up!" Mr. Dempsey starts yelling. "It's very slippery out here, there's water all over the floor! If you're supposed to be in class then get back to class. Kyle, you find Mr. Franklin please, and get some of those signs that tell you the floor is wet."

Nurse Kelly tosses open the door leading to the staircase and emerges from within.

"Careful, Melinda," Mr. Dempsey says over the girl's crying, holding his right arm up to slow her down, but then wincing. "Floor's all wet. The damn fountain is broken."

"These two are always messing with the fountain out here," Stewart says, "but never like this."

"Yeah, I'm not really sure what they're doing," I reply. "Should we try to stop them or something?"

"We really can't," answers Stewart, although he looks like he is trying to come up with a plan.

When Nurse Kelly reaches the girl, Mr. Dempsey wanders over to the fountain, unplugs it, and fiddles with a valve underneath it. It turns off, but the residuals don't budge from their positions.

"Stupid thing," he mumbles, looking back over at the girl.

"Call for an ambulance, please, Mark," Nurse Kelly says in an even tone while shooting him a serious look. He nods and walks back towards his classroom.

"What's going on?" I say, turning to Stewart.

"The residuals are freaking out," he replies. "It's not good." Then he runs a hand through his curls and sighs.

Margot

Margot sucks her breath in when she turns the corner of the hallway, and her heart races. Kimberley is waiting in front of her locker. She thinks about turning around, but Kimberley has spotted her and waves.

"Hey," Margot says as she approaches, forcing a smile.

"Hey," Kimberley replies, raising her eyebrows, and Margot swallows, feeling instantly defensive.

"What's up?"

"You tell me," Kimberley says.

"What do you mean?" Margot reaches for the lock on her locker and begins to spin the black dial.

"For a while I thought maybe the whole phone thing was too much for you because . . ." Kimberley stops and lowers her voice, "because of James. But then as I was trying to find you yesterday so that I could ask you again if you wanted to come to Hailey's house and hang out with us, I noticed you were on your phone. And waiting for *Douglas Arsenault.*" She says his name as if she's just taken a sip of sour milk. Margot snaps her lock open and stares ahead. "So what is it, Margot? Because it's clearly not that you're avoiding your phone anymore. And I know you got stuck with him as a lab partner that time when you were late to class, but the lab is over now."

"I'm just . . ." she pauses and opens the locker door. "I don't know."

"Everyone is worried about you. Your mom calls my mom a few times a week to see if I've told her anything about how you're doing. And Mrs. Burns is constantly on me to give her some details."

"Kim, I'm sorry. I'm not trying to make things tough for

you." Margot can feel the urge to cry sneaking up the back of her throat.

"I just don't get why you're avoiding us. We're your friends. People are getting to the point where they don't want to even try anymore, Margot."

"Awesome," she says flatly.

Kimberley throws her head back in exasperation. "No, not awesome. It's been months. We all know what you've been through, but it's like you don't even want to be friends with us anymore."

"That's not how I feel," Margot says quietly.

"Well, it seems like it. We can never find you. You ignore us. And when you do spend time with people it's with Douglas? You know he was there the night that Ali girl died, right?"

"Just stop,"

"I'm serious, he's frightening."

"He's not."

"Okay, well everyone thinks so except for you."

Margot shakes her head and rolls her eyes.

"I'm sorry. It's just been hard," she says after a few moments.

"We know that!"

"So what do you want then?" Margot asks, spinning around and staring at her.

"I don't know! Answer a text here or there. Find us at lunch. Stop avoiding us altogether!" Margot watches as Kimberley's eyes catch something behind her and she narrows them. She turns around to see that Douglas has made his way up behind them.

"Hey," he says, his eyes darting back and forth between the two of them. "I don't mean to interrupt."

"Perfect," Kimberley says, rolling her eyes. She turns around and walks in the other direction down the hallway.

"I'm sorry," Margot says as Douglas stares, wide-eyed. "She's just upset with me."

"Yeah, sorry if I made that worse somehow. I just wanted to see if you still wanted to hang out after school." He smiles at her, and she exhales loudly.

"I do," Margot says, closing her locker harder than necessary. "I definitely do."

"Can I tell you something?" Margot asks. Her body feels like a balloon that needs to be grounded to earth with a tether.

"Sure," says Douglas in a sleepy voice. They are lying in the grass on the levee, the river stretching out in front of them, bundled in blankets and basking in the glow of the magic hour light before sunset. Around them Frisbees are being thrown, conversations punctuated by laughter carry on, and she can still taste the last beer on her breath.

"It's going to sound a little crazy."

"'Kay."

"Promise you won't laugh?" she whispers.

"Promise," his voice says from a distant place.

"Sometimes, I think James is talking to me." Her statement is met with silence. "Are you still awake?"

"Yeah, I heard you."

"Do you think I'm insane?"

"No."

A Frisbee lands with a thud by their heads.

"Ugh," Douglas groans, propping himself up on one elbow and flipping it back to its owner. He then returns to his relaxed position.

"So? Did you hear what I said?" Margot asks, hating the slurry tone and needy nature of her question.

"Yeah. I said I did."

"Oh. I wasn't sure if you were sleeping or something." She watches a little girl do cartwheels in a straight line.

"I wasn't."

"And you don't think I'm nuts?"

"Well, I mean, are you hearing voices and shit?"

"No," Margot laughs a little too much. "No, not like that. I just mean giving me signs kinda thing."

"Oh, that's cool."

"Yeah. It kind of is." She sits up and looks at the river. An enormous barge is floating by. It blocks out the sun on its way.

"Does that ever happen to you?"

"What?"

"Like do you ever feel like Ali's trying to communicate with you somehow?" She rolls over and stares at his profile, pushes a strand of his hair to the side.

"No. Never. I'm not sure why she would even want to," he says without opening his eyes.

Margot nods. The sun is back.

"Shit. I forgot to take that antidepressant this morning."

"Just take two tomorrow or something," says Douglas, whose voice signals that he is succumbing to sleep.

"Yeah," she says softly.

Her phone buzzes from her pocket. A text from her mom: "Will you be home for dinner?"

"Will grab something with friends," she texts.

"Be home by 8. School night," is the reply. She rolls her eyes.

"K."

Douglas is breathing heavily now. She looks over at him and smiles. He looks like a baby on his stomach, arms curled up by his head. She feels a rush of affection for him, but then her thoughts turn back to James, and her posture shrinks.

It's you, isn't it? she thinks, looking up at the sky. It has to be you. Somehow. She smiles and turns her gaze back to the river.

James

I shift in my chair and stare at the blinking clock on the microwave. I wasn't going to come to this meeting, but Stewart saw me in the hallway on my way to the library and said he thought we should all meet today, that there is a lot of stuff going on. I passed Ali on the way and asked if she was coming, but she is busy touching a girl's head repeatedly as she talks to a group of friends. The girl scratches and moves her hair around.

"Making them suspect lice," she smirks. I just smile and keep walking.

So here I am. I cross my arms and lean back in the chair before Stewart reminds me to put it down on the floor. I really want to get to the library before fourth period and get to the book, so I am hoping this goes quickly.

"Hey," Gabriella says breezing in and sitting down at the table. "Ali coming?"

I shrug and look over at the door.

"Anyway," says Stewart. "I was here early morning for the coffee rush and I overheard a few things that might be useful to know."

"Sure, what do you have?" Gabriella asks, turning her head towards him.

"Well, Tom McCarthy got caught cheating on his history test. He's suspended for two days."

"Nothing new there," I say. "Only the fact that he got caught."

"Okay, I guess I was just wondering if there was something putting stress on him, causing him to cheat."

"If there is, it's the same thing that's been putting stress on him for years, so it might not be worth worrying about," I say as Ali rushes in and sits down in the chair next to me.

"Sorry I'm late."

"No problem," says Stewart.

"What else do you have?" Gabriella asks.

"Well, Mrs. Turner, the art teacher, is friends with Hannah Lincoln's mom. Sounds like the last round of chemo did not work like they hoped it would."

"Oh, that's too bad." Gabriella grimaces. "I've been watching her, and she's so down. Did either of you know her?" she asks, glancing at me and Ali.

"No," I say.

"I knew of her," says Ali. "But we weren't friends."

"Yeah, she's definitely someone we should keep an eye on," says Stewart. "And anything we can do to make her day a little easier we should."

"Anyone else have anything?"

"Well, I know James is concerned about his friend, Margot, but what have you seen with Douglas?" Gabriella says, stretching out the words.

I look up at her and narrow my eyes. The table is quiet. I wonder about mentioning Mr. Firenze and the note and police, but I don't. I've covered my bases with that kid. Reminded him to keep his appointment.

Instead, I say, "Yeah, of course I'm worried about Margot, but I'm on that."

Stewart looks back and forth between Gabriella and I and then nods.

"Her name hasn't come up in graffiti for anyone, right?" asks Gabriella, looking at each of them. Ali just stares back and Stewart shakes his head.

"And that means I can't be worried about her?" I ask, making an effort not to raise my voice.

"Of course not, James," Stewart says. "You know we're happy to keep an eye on her too if you feel like she needs it."

"And Douglas?" Gabriella asks.

"What about him?" I say. "He's basically on probation here and miserable."

Ali clears her throat and Gabriella nods and looks towards the door. Mrs. Garcia has just entered, coffee cup in one hand.

I look over toward the wall, remembering Mrs. Garcia's sensitivity to Dan's pipe. Then I look up at the clock on the wall.

"Hey, where's Dan?" I ask.

"Good question," Stewart says, frowning and staring at the chair. He looks up at the clock. "It is about the time we usually see him." He and Gabriella exchange worried glances.

"Maybe he overslept today," Ali says. "Had to go out for some more tobacco."

"Well, that's actually another reason I thought we should all meet today," says Stewart. He clears his throat. "I am getting concerned."

"About Dan?" I ask.

"About them in general."

"The residuals," Gabriella says when I still look confused.

"Why would we be concerned about them?" Ali asks.

Gabriella sighs. "Because they follow the same bursts of leftover energy all the time. If they start doing different things, well . . . that means something has shifted. There are different energy paths."

"What could possibly shift?" I say over Mrs. Garcia's sudden humming. "We're dead, they're dead."

"It's hard to explain," Stewart says. "It has to do with balance."

I shake my head. "I don't get it."

"Yeah, I'm confused too," says Ali.

"If something is upsetting the energy here, the balance, and they don't just do their same mundane, harmless things every day, then the things that they will start doing can harm people. Like the other day with that poor girl breaking her leg in a couple of places because they flooded the hallway. Maybe it was just a weird fluke, but now Dan's not here. They just seem off."

My mind jumps to Nick suddenly falling on the track. I uncross my arms and straighten my posture.

"What?" says Gabriella, staring at me and narrowing her eyes. "What is it?"

The look of agony on Nick's face races through my thoughts, the vision of his coach running over to him. I'm not sure if I want to share it. Something about it feels private.

"Um, nothing. I guess I'm just processing it."

"Why would they just suddenly act weird?" Ali asks.

"There are a lot of possibilities," says Stewart. "When the living start to sense that we're here because we've been careless it can trigger an imbalance. I triggered it once early on with Mr. Franklin. I'd be going about my business later in the day, moving stuff around, forgetting he was still on campus. I was able to correct it pretty quickly once we figured it out."

"There can be other stuff too," Gabriella adds. "But it's complicated. Let's just watch it. Everyone make sure we're being careful. Make sure if you get a mission, you do it. Make sure we're following all the rules." I see her try to meet Ali's eyes, but Ali is looking at the ground.

"Let's try to come together every morning for the next little while too," says Stewart. "I think it's important that we keep sharing what we see."

"But what does it all mean?" I ask. I look around the table at the different expressions: Stewart's unjudgmental but concerned one, Gabriella's suspicious one, and Ali's hopeful one. I shake my head.

"There's something I didn't mention in there," I tell Ali after we leave the faculty lounge. "Douglas is getting notes."

"I heard about the note in the principal's office," Ali says. "I'm glad they're reopening it. I hate it for my parents, but if they put more pressure on him, maybe he'll give Clinton up." She walks directly through a puddle from a spilled water bottle. I stop and put it right-side up and then jog to join her again.

"Why do you think he hasn't before?"

"Because Clinton scares the crap out of him. And because god forbid Douglas does anything right."

"Do you ever think maybe you're being a little hard on him? I mean, believe me, I am not a fan, but he didn't kill you, Ali." She stops, and her head whips around. I feel her eyes fixate on me.

"Do you feel sorry for him, James?" she asks, crossing her arms. "Please tell me that you don't feel sorry for him."

"No, I don't feel sorry for him," I say. I lift my head and return the stare.

"That's good, because you're definitely not going to feel sorry for him when he inevitably messes with Margot's head too."

I sigh and rub my temples. "I'm trying to make sense of things. I just know that I don't want to stay."

She starts walking again. "I already told you that you don't have to."

"And I hope you're right. But the only things I know are that I can move on by doing what the graffiti tells me to do, or I can follow whatever directions you get from 'them.' So, I'm covering my bases. Anyway, it's not just that one note." We walk through the doors that lead to her favorite space by the tree. It's a sunny day, and I notice a little green lizard sitting on the warm concrete of the steps as I follow her down them.

"Oh yeah?"

"Yeah. There are ones that are just to him. I've seen him get a couple."

"And?" She's under the shade of the tree now and turns to face me.

"And are you sure that's going to accomplish anything?"

"What I hope it accomplishes is that he thinks about how he left me there with that horrible human being. I hope that he thinks to himself that even if we were fighting a little, he should have helped me get home. And that if he did, I might still be there living my life. And what I really hope is that someday, somehow, he finds it in himself to tell the police the truth about what happened to me."

I nod. "I understand."

"Good, I am glad *you're* not lecturing me about leaving notes." She sits down and smiles up at me.

Margot

Margot stares into the mirror of the second-floor bathroom. The face looking back at her is pale, she can barely see her freckles, and there are light purple semicircles underneath her eyes. She sighs, but the truth is she doesn't really care. The antidepressants are helping more than she would have thought. It's like the sadness is a layer deep down that you know is there but would take a shovel to get out. Combined with her other pills, they are doing the trick. She'll be out of her secret ones soon though. She might have to ask Douglas if he knows where she can get more.

She turns her head from side to side, examining both angles. She runs her fingers through her hair. Good enough, she thinks and turns to leave.

"Oh hi," says Lucy Simons as she walks into the bathroom, initially startled by Margot's presence and then switching over to that same deer in the headlights look that most people seem to get around her.

"Hey," says Margot, forcing a weak smile.

Lucy pauses as if she might say something, then returning the smile, she stares down at the ground and walks to a bathroom stall. Margot shifts her backpack to a different shoulder and makes her way out.

Douglas is absent, so she decides that she will just grab a sandwich and sit outside by herself. The cafeteria is loud and all of the food smells sour to her. When she gets in line with her sandwich, she sees Lucy standing with Kimberley and Hailey, talking with her hands and pulling her eyes down like a zombie. Hailey looks up and notices her watching. A panicked look crosses her face and she turns away, shaking her head at Lucy to stop.

Outside Margot sits on a patch of grass soaking up the sun and tearing off tiny pieces of the sandwich that she pops in her mouth. She pictures the girls hanging on every word as Lucy tells them about seeing her in the bathroom. She has become used to people not knowing how to deal with her anymore, but ripping on her appearance is new. She tosses the sandwich down next to her and stretches out, tilting her head towards the sunny sky and trying to fight off tears.

She has half of one of her other pills in her backpack. She was going to save it until after school, but now she thinks she might just go ahead and take it. Blow off afternoon classes. At least that way she won't spend the rest of the afternoon remembering the horrified looks on their faces and the reflection that was looking back at her in the mirror.

James

"You're here early," I say to Ali as I walk into the teachers' lounge.

"I wanted to beat the rush," she replies, slamming shut one of the flimsy, cream-colored cabinets by the sink and looking at the door behind me. "Did you see any teachers?"

I shake my head. "Why?"

"Just doing the regular to decaf switch."

I nod and she reaches for a white coffee filter.

She turns around and smiles at me as the machine clicks on and sputters as it begins to drip hot coffee into the pot.

I smile back at her and say, "I wanted to ask if you had heard more about, you know . . . Going back."

"Shhh!" she hisses. "Let's talk outside."

"So?" I ask when we get outside to the tree. She sits down and props herself up against the trunk. She seems suddenly tired and unwilling to hold a conversation. Her eyes, which she closes, flutter open and then close again.

"I can go soon. That's really all I know."

"Just you?"

"Are you saying that you want to go, James?"

"Yes. I think I do."

"You *think* you do?" She snaps a twig she has been playing with.

"I meant I do. I thought about it a lot last night. There's no reason for me to stay here. I'm useless."

"That's not what Gabriella and Stewart would tell you."

"I know that. And I don't agree with them."

"Right. You need to be sure though, is what I am saying. There are things at stake."

"Like what?"

"You know, just that whole messing with the order thing." She shrugs. "But you already know all about that."

My stomach dips a little.

"It's okay, James, I'm not going to tell them," she says and looks over at me. I try to ignore her smirk.

"So, is this like reincarnation? We could come back as starving babies in a third world country? Or even a bug or something?"

"No!" she rolls her eyes. "It's not like that at all."

"How do you know?"

"I just know. It's going back at the same level you left at. In the place you left."

"And you trust them?"

She nods. "They haven't been wrong yet. Plus, what's the worst-case scenario? I die and get stuck here? Not much further to fall, if you know what I mean."

"But what if you go back and your new life is worse than your old one? Or even worse than being here?"

"Can't happen."

I shake my head. "I don't see how you can guarantee it. You could get stuck with an awful family."

"Think about it, James," she says with a hint of exasperation. "You can't just appear to a family as a sixteen-year-old child they never had before and suddenly start living as their son and attending school here."

"Yeah, I guess I hadn't thought it through to that point. So, how does it work then?"

We are quiet for a moment. Ali closes her eyes again.

"So, how does this work?" I ask again. "How do we do it?"

"I don't know. I just know they'll set it all up. In terms of getting there, there's a crossing point. I don't know where it is yet."

"Will you know soon?"

She nods. "I should. They said I would."

For a minute I allow myself to daydream about my new life. How I'd befriend Margot. How I'd visit all the places I loved in the city again. I wonder if I could ever meet my parents.

"I'm actually . . ." I pause. "I'm actually really ready for it."

"I know. It's going to be good. I'm *not* going to mess it up this time."

"What are you going to do?"

"I'm going to get into a kick ass college. I'm going to be the best cello player I can be. I'm going to try to maybe help my parents somehow. I don't know how I am going to do that, but I want to." She bites down on her lip and stares off.

"I'm going to help Margot. And I'm going to run. I'm really going to push myself there. I'm going to pull my grades up and hopefully get in a really good premed program. And I know what you mean about the parents."

"What's the first thing you'd eat?" I ask, sitting straight up and crossing my legs at my ankles.

"Um, beignets."

"Really?"

"Really. I love them. You?"

"I don't know. Too many options there."

"Pick one!" Her voice is animated and playful.

"Okay, a shrimp po' boy from Domilise's."

"Fair enough. I might meet you there after beignets."

We are both laughing now.

"Uh, she's so creepy," Ali says suddenly.

"Who is?"

"Gabriella. She keeps peeking out here. Like I don't see her or something."

"Where?" I glance over at the school.

"She's gone now. I think she knows that I saw her."

"I just don't get it."

"Get what?"

"Why they stay."

She shrugs and closes her eyes again.

That evening just the security lights are on in the library. I take my time walking in the dim light. I'm not in a rush to leave this message. The usual excitement I feel before picking the perfect passage isn't fluttering around in my stomach. I know what needs to be said.

The green pencil is still on Margot's last message. I remove it and begin to flip. My eyes scan for words in the text, and when I find it, I sigh.

God knows what you've been doing, everything you've been doing."

The words underlined, I insert the green pencil bookmark and close the book.

Margot

Margot's eyes shoot open then blink to focus on the faded pink of her bedroom walls. The cocoon she has created with her flowered comforter is too hot, and she peels it off the top half of her body and then lays motionless. The beagle next door is barking its sharp consecutive yaps. Her head starts to throb in unison. After a period of stillness it isn't a feeling of dread or guilt that starts to creep in and makes her chest tighten with anxiety. It is anger.

She hadn't left a return quote. She wasn't even going to check if the damn pencil was in the book on Monday.

"And it's probably not even you," she says into the still air of her bedroom, just in case he can hear her somehow. The phlegmy sound of her voice disgusts her.

She swallows. Her throat is dry and sharp, and the stale taste of tobacco in her mouth serves as the bookmark from which to start piecing together the evening's memories.

She smiles, recalling Douglas, slumped on the couch, his speech slurry, a baseball hat pulled down close to his eyes.

"You make things better," he had been trying to say. But the music in the garage where they had all congregated was loud, and her head was light from the beer and the heat. She thought he had said something about butter.

"What did you say?" She laughed, taking a dishonest drag of his cigarette and flicking her hair to one side. She leaned over him. When he struggled to enunciate it perfectly for her, his earnest expression made her laugh.

He leaned back, letting the couch swallow him and grinning with his eyes closed at the sound of her laughter.

She plopped down next to him. She knew she was drunk and laughing harder than the situation warranted, but something about the abandon of it all, her shoulders shaking, the warmth spreading to her cheeks, had felt too good to let go of. His arm pulled her in, and she had continued to laugh, her head buried in his chest.

Her mother is stirring in the kitchen below her. She'll have to wait for the sound of her exiting out the door for church before she gets up so that she can go deal with the hangover in peace. Church. She can't remember the last time she's been.

When the door slams and the sounds of the car pulling out of the driveway become clear, she swings her feet over the bed. Before standing, she pauses in anticipation of the new headache that will take over once she is upright.

In the kitchen, the smell of eggs hits her first. Her mother always loves to have eggs on Sunday. The smell of them combined with the sight of her mother's beloved green "super juice" coating the side of a glass cup on the counter make her gag a little.

In the fridge, she is happy to see a brand-new bottle of Coke sitting on the top shelf. That was another thing that ended when James died, her mother's ban on soft drinks. She is the queen of small comforts.

She sips on a glass of Coke and stares out the window at the street. The book, the pencil, the marked quote invade her already sore head.

The words rattle around her brain. *"God knows what you've been doing, everything you've been doing."*

She slams the glass down on the counter.

"How would you even know that anyway?" she yells at the ceiling.

The next day she almost didn't respond to it. Whoever is playing this game with her seems to be watching her closely. But why? When she racks her brain she can't come up with even one kid in the school who might care enough to monitor what she is doing. For a moment she even considers it might be Burns, trying to work with her through some crazy method. But this is too clever for Burns. She has considered a few angry responses, too, but since she can't be sure of the target of them, she tries to keep it light.

"Once in a while I go off on a spree and make a fool of myself, but I always come back."

James

I have to admit, the last quote was a good response. I actually smiled when I read it, but I also recognized the blow-off. So tonight I sit at the library table with my head in my hands, thinking about the type of reply I want to leave. I can't hint at how bad she looks. That would just upset her. I can't be too harsh, that might shut everything down.

I leaf through the book. Suddenly I feel that I am being watched, and when I look up I see Mr. Franklin, the janitor, staring in through the window with his mouth open. I freeze and stare back at him, wondering for a moment if he can see me before realizing that he's watching the pages of the book move.

"Crap," I think. "I should have checked to see if his car was gone." I'd been so eager to respond to Margot that I'd been more careless than usual.

I panic and shut the book but immediately regret it. The man's eyes widen, and he takes two steps backward from the glass. I freeze. Mr. Franklin starts shaking his head slowly and walks away.

When he's out of sight I grab the book and run to the stacks with it. I sit on the ground and continue to thumb through it, trying to refocus after the encounter. She can't see me, but I can hear Gabriella calling my name from the other side of the library. I ignore her.

It takes me much longer than usual, but I'm happy when I finally settle on it. I underline, "*I realized by some unmistakable sign that an intimate revelation was quivering on the horizon,*" and put it back on the shelf.

The next morning I notice that the door of the teachers' lounge is framed with thick red tinsel. Inside a couple of teachers are sporting holiday sweaters and tacky earrings shaped like candy canes or presents. The refrigerator has a flyer on the door that reads, "Christmas Concert Thursday Night!"

"I hadn't even thought about Christmas," I say out loud, staring at the flyer. Teachers chatter behind me. I think of my house at this time of year. The tree in the foyer. The white lights on the fence. The fake holly wreath with the giant red ribbon on it that my mom puts on the door. Will all those things make it up this year? My head sinks, and I stare at the ground.

"Hey," says Gabriella as she comes through the door. "How's it going?"

"I forgot all about Christmas," I respond.

"Really?" She smiles, walking towards me. "There are decorations everywhere!"

"Yeah, I know. I guess I just wasn't paying attention."

"You okay?" she asks, squinting at me.

"I guess so. I was just thinking of my parents."

She nods. "They'll be okay," she says and pats me on the back.

I turn my head away from her and roll my eyes. How does she know that? How does she know that there will be a tree or lights or a wreath on the door?

But that's not what she meant, and I know it. She meant it's part of what's supposed to happen to them too. And that it's okay that they're going through it right now. She meant it's okay if there's no Christmas at their house this year, or if there is. I've heard it from her so much at this point, about the order of things.

"There'll be many peaceful moments around this place, though," Gabriella says. "You'd think it'd be lonely, but in a lot of ways it's really beautiful."

Another thing I hadn't thought of—the students all being gone. I close my eyes and cover my face with my hands as I realize that I won't be able to keep tabs on Margot.

"James," Gabriella says, leaning in as a teacher breezes by us and starts making copies. The machine fills the room with a hum and loud whooshing noises as it spits out paper. "James, your parents are going to be okay. Remember, they will find a way through not having you there anymore. I promise."

I nod, but my thoughts turn to what Margot will do with all that free time.

"Have you seen Stewart yet?" she asks, glancing up at the clock.

"I saw him earlier this morning but not since I've been in here."

"Something must have held him up. What about Ali?" I shake my head.

"I wish she'd stop in too. I want to know if anyone's seen any more weird stuff with the residuals."

"Like I said, haven't seen her."

"James, you don't think she's . . ."

I look over at her with an expectant look on my face, waiting for her to finish her sentence. She shifts around a little. "She's what?"

"Like getting too close to them or something. Maybe pranks going a little too far? Raising their suspicions type of thing."

"I haven't seen it. I mean, I don't spend that much time with her."

"I just don't get it," she whispers. "Something has got to be triggering them." Her blue eyes stare off towards the door.

"Is it possible that sometimes they can just act weird without a reason?" I try to make my voice sound as neutral as possible.

She scrunches up her face. "I've never seen it."

"Is it really that big a deal?" I walk over to the counter by the sink and sweep away some loose coffee grounds that are bothering me then turn back around to face her.

"It can be," she says. "It can get a lot worse than a broken leg."

I raise my eyebrows and lean back against the counter.

"Do you feel like you're being careful on your missions?"

"Yeah. I mean, I really have only had the one."

"Well, we just have to be careful. There's a trigger somewhere." She stares off into the distance again and then says, "I'll be back. I'm going to see if I can find Stewart."

"Good luck," I say as she leaves.

I sit and think about everything for a minute. I miss knowing what is true and what is not. Having clarity.

"Screw it," I say and stand to leave. I also miss not having to think so much about every damn thing. As I walk out of the teachers' lounge, I practically walk into two policemen.

"Yeah," one of the men says to the other, scratching the side of his face where I bumped into him. "So, we start when they're back from the break then. Locker searches too."

When I get to the tree, I start to tell Ali about the policemen, but she interrupts me.

"James, there's something I haven't told you about going back," she says. "I wasn't going to tell you this, but since you're seriously considering it now, I think you should know."

"What is it?" I turn my head towards her but she is looking off into the distance.

"There's more to it than just making the decision to go."

"Like what?" A police car passes by, and she waits until the siren is no longer blaring.

"The protectors will take replacements."

"I don't know what that means." I shake my head.

"For us. They will take replacements for us."

"What do you mean? Take them from where?" I shrug and try to meet her eyes.

"Other students, James. I mean they'll take other students. To be here instead of us," she whispers.

"What? Why? Why would they do that?" I edge closer to her.

"They wouldn't want to. But we'd be forcing their hand." She looks at me, bites down on her bottom lip, and looks back towards the school.

"I still don't get it."

"Because they'll need to maintain their power. Keep the balance."

"And you've decided you're okay with that?"

"I have." She nods and meets my eyes.

"How?"

"Because who cares about them, James?" She points at the school. "Why are their lives, their hopes and dreams, more important than mine?"

"And why are the whispers okay with that?" I ask, narrowing my eyes. "Why would they be okay with us coming back and two other people having to die?"

"Because they don't believe in what protectors do."

"Why? Aren't they—*we*—just here to try to help people?"

"Maybe," she says raising her voice, "but I'm convinced there are other things Stewart and Gabriella don't tell us. Besides, they kind of suck at it, don't they?"

I sigh and stand up, stare at the windows of the classrooms full of students.

"They didn't do a damn thing for me," she continues. "I'm not sure how they missed it! I couldn't have stuck out more if I had tried! And I don't understand the complete randomness of it anyway! Think about it. Why are you supposed to help Douglas but nobody is supposed to look out for Margot?"

"I still don't understand," I say.

"If we're back on the other side we can help them. Eventually, we'd be able to edge protectors out. People would move on—truly move on—when it's time. They believe in do-overs. Protectors don't."

"But how does us going back help the whispers?"

"It's about balance. Eventually if there is more energy on their side, protectors are overwhelmed."

"I'm still not sure I understand." I tilt my head up at the sky and look at the clouds.

"I don't get all of it right now either. I don't think we'll know all of it until we get back. But I do know that it's better than sitting here every day."

I may not understand everything that she is talking about, but I am pretty sure she is right about that.

Margot

School is officially out for the holidays and Margot is suffering through dinner with her mother. Elaine Cramer has made her daughter's favorite, spaghetti and meatballs, only to watch Margot roll the meatballs over the pasta and take sporadic, birdlike bites. They sit across from each other at the little bistro table in the corner of the kitchen, which Elaine has tried to make cheerful with a fresh bouquet of flowers. Their scent is overpowering though and is competing with the food.

"How was the last day before the break?"

Margot shrugs.

Have you been able to meet with Mrs. Burns when you need to?"

"Here and there." Margot shakes some Parmesan cheese over her spaghetti. She watches as the white flakes absorb the sauce and turn pink. "It's not like it's helpful."

"It's not?" her mother says, furrowing her brow and then taking a bite of food. She watches Margot as she chews and then says, "I thought you liked Mrs. Burns. Do you feel like we should look for someone outside of the school?"

"No." Margot stares at her plate.

"Well, I want you to have someone you feel like you can talk with, Margot."

"I'm okay, Mom. I don't really feel like this is something I can just talk out."

"No, of course not. Talking about it is not going to make everything go away, but it can make it easier here and there."

Margot rolls her eyes. "That's the point, Mom. There is no easier."

"I just think it's important," her mother says in a whispered tone.

"Burns is fine." Margot pokes a small bowl of salad with her fork and eventually harpoons a spinach leaf to eat. They are quiet for a few minutes. The oven timer beeps and her mother rises, heels clacking across the kitchen floor, to retrieve a loaf of garlic bread.

"Well, how are your classes going?" she asks, sitting back down.

"I'm doing my best."

"I'm sure you are. I know it's difficult."

Margot nods. Elaine Cramer has to look away at the wall and focus on something else for a moment. There are times when the mask of grief that seems to engulf her daughter's face is just too much to bear looking at. She wonders if joy will ever come back and animate it.

"You're not hungry?" she asks as Margot twists spaghetti around her fork but never lifts it to her mouth.

"I thought I was. I had some snacks after school. I must have filled up."

"Well, I can put this in some Tupperware. Maybe you can eat some more of it tomorrow."

"Yeah, thanks. I'm actually kind of tired, Mom. I may go lay down."

Her mother twists her mouth up a little but nods. She makes a mental note to call the pediatrician Monday about the depression and exhaustion.

Margot grabs her backpack from where she had dropped it when she walked in the door.

"You're doing homework?" her mother asks. "It's Friday and you're on vacation!"

"Oh," Margot says with a small smile. "I know. I have a free reading book in here. I was going to read before bed."

"Okay. Go rest, sweetheart," her mom says, dabbing at her face with a napkin and forcing a smile.

"Thanks."

Margot hadn't checked the book out. She'd just taken it from the library, afraid that if she borrowed it she'd be accused of defacing it when it got returned. And she didn't want to lose track of all that underlining. She wants to be able to read it over and over again whenever she needs to.

When she reaches her room, she sets the novel down on her white desk and stares at it. It is weathered, and the middle bulges from where the green pencil is wedged in it. The sight of it makes her smile, but it also looks strange here in her room and not on the shelf at the library in its usual spot.

She reaches out her hand and touches it. She doesn't know what she was expecting. Some special feeling to radiate from the book through her hand? She wants so badly to believe it is James. Who else could it be, really? Who else would bother with such a back-and-forth with her?

She pulls the desk chair out and sits down. Her eyes are heavy; she hasn't been lying to her mother that she wants to go to bed. Even when Douglas had tried to talk her into coming out tonight she had declined. Something about all the holiday clamor at school had exhausted her. The decorations, the cheerfulness, classes that teachers just let devolve into chaotic chat sessions because energy was bubbling over and they realized that they could not hold everyone's attention for a regular class.

She opens the book and scans. Will it be like Santa Claus? She'll have to be asleep for him to come? What if she wakes up and sees him? God, what if that happened?

She shakes her head and focuses on the pages in front of her. Her eyes feel blurry, but she scans the pages back and forth. She underlines: *"I was alone again in the unquiet darkness."*

James

I flick on the light in the library when I walk in because I can. Mr. Franklin and the rest of the after-hours people are home with their families, I am sure. I picture Mr. Franklin around a table full of people, out of his uniform and enjoying a big meal. As I walk my mind starts to wander off towards the scene at my own house, and I shut it down immediately as I get to the shelf.

I see the blank space in front of me and reach my hand out towards it before I realize what it means. The book is not there. I feel around to see if it's just been pushed in too far or if it's tipped over. Then I scan the titles of all the books around the spot to see if it was put back in the wrong place, but it's not. It's gone. I look everywhere for it—on nearby shelves, in the book return, on random carts around the library. I can't find it anywhere. As I stand in the library glancing all around through the security lighting and trying to decide where to look next, panic starts to ripple through me. What if *they* found it? What if they know?

I decide to feel the situation out so I head towards the outside lounge. As I cross through the gym doors, I hear Gabriella say, "For right now we're just lucky that the students aren't here. We've got to try to fix this before they come back."

"What's up?" I ask as they both glance over at me.

"Oh, hey James," Gabriella says, her voice sounding deflated. Stewart lifts his hand in a wave and gives me a small smile.

"Something wrong?" I ask, watching her face carefully.

"Sort of," she says.

"Residuals," Stewart chimes in. "We officially have a problem."

"What do you mean?" I ask.

"Something's upset them," Gabriella says, staring at me. "And we can't find the trigger."

I look away and then say, "Well, what do you think it is?"

"Don't know, but we need to figure it out. Today one of them started a small fire in the kitchen," Stewart says. "I happened to be walking through to go check on something in the back parking lot. I watched one of them turn on a burner on the big stove. Almost caught the edge of a rag someone left on the counter. It's getting dangerous now."

I nod. "What can we do?" I ask.

"Just be observant," says Gabriella, and I swear it feels like her eyes are going right through me.

"Sure," I say. "Yeah, of course."

"I'm going to go walk around a little," says Stewart, standing and starting to walk towards the doors. "Keep my eye out."

"I'll probably walk around a little too," I say.

"Great, thanks James," Gabriella says, still looking at me. I nod, smile, and follow Stewart inside.

"I'm going to head this way," I say, pointing to the right as we exit the gym. He waves as he heads in the opposite direction.

Ali is out by the tree.

"Residuals are freaking out," I say as I sit down next to her. She is laying on her stomach, her head resting on her arms.

"What do you mean?" she asks, sounding as though her thoughts are somewhere else.

"Stewart says they tried to start a fire."

"Stewart says?"

"Well, yeah. Why do you say it like that?" I ask.

"Those things have always creeped me out a little anyway," she says. "If they're here, why aren't they just one of us?"

"What do you think is wrong with them?" I pick up a twig and bend it to see how far it can go before snapping.

"Who knows, James. What did Stewart and Gabriella say again? Something about their balance being thrown off?"

We are quiet, and I look up at the stars.

"The book is gone," I say. "Can't find it anywhere."

"Oh yeah?"

"Yeah. I can't figure it out."

"Why do you think it's lost?"

"Because it's not where I left it," I say, irritated.

"Just asking," she says, shooting me a look and sitting up. "Have they seen you with it?"

"I don't think so. Why?" I ask, trying hard to keep my face from showing how nervous I am getting.

"You should be more careful, James. But because I feel you wondering, I didn't tell them about it. And I didn't take it."

I open my mouth to speak but decide against it.

"And I doubt they did either or they'd be all over you about it. Anyway, it's fine," she says, smiling. "I get it. We're not like them. We're not emotionless robots. And I'm not ever going to say anything to them about it."

"Okay," I say softly and look down.

"But if I had to guess, James," she says while leaning in to make eye contact. "It's you or me that is upsetting the balance."

I nod.

"And I don't know what they'd do if they found that out."

"I'm not going to say anything either," I whisper.

"Pinky swear," she says and holds out her hand. We lock fingers.

"Have you heard anything?" I ask as she stretches out again.

"Nothing specific to what you're talking about."

"I'm ready," I say. My words hang in the air waiting for me to second guess them but instead I just say them again silently in my head.

Margot

Margot had fallen asleep almost instantly after climbing into bed in a pair of sweatpants and an old track team tee-shirt that had belonged to James. She wakes to the sound of the neighbor's dog.

It's light outside. The air in her room is cold, and she pulls the blanket up towards her ears and shuts her eyes again. She can hear the faint buzzing of her phone on her nightstand, making small rattling noises against the wood. She tries to ignore it, but it's no use. She is awake.

She blinks her eyes several times and rolls over. After a minute she stretches out her arm and grabs the phone. Douglas. Three new messages.

"party at rachels. come out."

"ignoring me?"

The third is a picture of him making a sad face and holding up a plastic cup of beer. Margot smiles. She taps at the screen and replies, "sorry just saw these. fell asleep crazy early."

She looks at the time. 8:26 am. She stares at the picture for a minute, smiling until the memory of the book on her desk bursts through her thoughts.

She puts the phone down in slow motion and stares over at the desk as she sits up. She swallows and blinks. What if there is a new underlining? What will she do? She peels the blankets off and takes a deep breath, swinging her feet to the floor.

Her heart pounds. She steps toward the book and stares down at it. It looks undisturbed, but there is really only one way to tell. Her hands touch the side of the book, looking for the gap in the paper where the pencil rests.

When she finds it, she flips it over without hesitating. The echo of her heartbeat fills her head, and it is a moment before she can focus on the text.

The same exact passage that she had underlined stares up at her. It isn't him. It is totally someone at school. She puts her hands on her head and stares up at the ceiling, then exhales.

"I am such an idiot," she says out loud, a small nervous laugh following. Her eyes begin to well. "I am such a total idiot."

James

My thoughts are running around my head along with the sound of Ali's cello. She told me earlier that the holiday vacations are her favorite because there is truly nobody around, and I can see it on her face. Her eyes are closed, and she sways slightly as she plays.

I wonder if Margot has gone to see her dad at all. Every once in a while she'll fly to New York City over the holidays. It's usually the same pattern. She starts off excited about all of the things she's going to do—skating in Rockefeller Center, tea at the Plaza, museums—then a couple of days in, when her dad has gone back to work, she calls more, and I pretend that I don't hear the pang of disappointment in her voice.

"Haven't gotten to the museum yet. I do love it here, though." She'd repeat the last part a few times during phone conversations.

"I know you do. New Yorker Margot."

"Maybe someday," she'd reply.

I shake my head to be done with the memory.

"Do you think it's my fault?" I ask Ali as she takes a break and her shoulders slump a little.

"Yes," she smiles and turns her head to me. "Joking. I have no idea what you are talking about. Do I think what is your fault?"

"The residual stuff."

"Possible," she says. "Could be either of us though."

I lean back in the metal chair and sigh.

"It's not your fault you have feelings, James. We can't help that we're not numb, that something didn't stick."

"But what if that's selfish? What if that's putting other people, maybe even the people we care about, in danger?"

She shrugs. "I seriously doubt that's the case. A girl slipped and broke her leg. Sucks for her, but I don't think it means everything is falling apart. Plus, there are not that many people I care about here." She smirks.

"And the fire. They're definitely acting weird. Have you seen it?"

"Maybe a little. I never paid all that much attention to them anyway. I don't need an extra daily reminder of my current state."

"Well, I've seen it," I say. I look down at my feet and think of Nick's fall on the track.

"I wouldn't worry about it. Nothing the two of them can't handle, I'm sure." She flips the pages around in the book on the music stand.

"I'm going to go lie down on the bleachers," I say, standing up just as she raises her bow to begin to play, and she nods without looking at me. I am not sure why, but deep down I feel it is all my fault, and I'm scared about what I might have done.

Margot

Margot wants the library to feel the same, but it doesn't. It used to make her feel safe, like a shell that a turtle could retreat into whenever it felt threatened, but now it just leaves her feeling exposed.

She has just come from lunch off campus with Douglas, and on the walk back she allowed herself to smoke pot for the second time. The first time was over Christmas break at Jack Delaney's house, but she barely felt it. This time a couple of small puffs were enough to make her feel like someone had massaged the tension out of her shoulders, but her eyes and her mouth feel dry. She struggles to remember if there is a water fountain in the library.

She pauses and looks in both directions as she walks in through the double doors. She pretends to reposition her backpack and then looks around again. Whoever is underlining the book knows when she is there. Knows when she has underlined something herself. There is a boy in an armchair in the corner, engrossed in a book. He doesn't even look up from it when he raises his arm to scratch his head. On the other side of the library, Elise Daniels and Lucy Lambert sit at a table, notebooks spread out around them. She suspects them for a moment since she'd seen them there a lot, and she narrows her eyes at them as they whisper back and forth to each other, wide-eyed and smiling, oblivious to Margot's stare.

"Nah, they wouldn't care enough to do that," she reasons. She tucks her thumbs underneath the straps of her backpack and looks around some more.

"There are open work tables in the back," Ms. Perez says

from the circulation desk, waving at her and then pointing towards the back where Margot always goes anyway.

She nods and forces a smile.

"What does it really matter anyway?" she asks herself as she walks toward the gray metal shelves filled with novels. "It was just a game, and I let myself believe it because I wanted to." She chastised herself so many times over the break, every time she was alone in her room and the tears and disappointment took over. How had she ever let herself believe it was anything more than a stupid game with some other *The Great Gatsby* nut? And there's definitely more than one chewed green pencil in the world.

She walks down the aisle and unzips her black backpack, staring at the book for a moment before putting it back on the shelf. She lets her hand linger on it and takes a deep breath.

"I'm so dumb," she whispers, shaking her head. She takes a couple of steps backward and stares at the sight of it back in its rightful place instead of torturing her on her desk at home. As she stares, a lazy, stoned, tight-lipped smirk takes over her face.

She has already left a quote for her fellow gamer. *"Well, there I was, way off on my ambitions . . . and all of a sudden I didn't care."*

James

I never thought she'd take it with her. I'm not sure why that thought never occurred to me. Maybe I am so used to my own confinement here that I forgot the book didn't have to stay too. But the Monday that the students return I follow her into the library and watch as she takes it out of her backpack. She holds it in her hands and shakes it a bit as she smiles, and I feel like I have been punched in the gut by what I see in her eyes.

Biting her lip a little, like she is holding in a laugh, she walks it over to the shelf and taps it into the empty space. She looks over her shoulder and then glances from side to side before she walks away. I stay and stare down the aisle, and after a little while I just sit down on the ground.

My mind races. I've lost her. On one hand, if I am responsible for everything with the residuals, maybe it's a good thing. But how am I going to get through my days here without Margot to focus on?

I must have nodded off because my eyes flutter open and I am on the floor watching Ms. Perez's feet walk by as she calls, "Library is closing. Anyone still working please start to pack up."

I stare up at the book, waiting until the long rows of lights in the ceiling start to flicker off before I grab it. I laugh when I see what she's underlined.

After some page turning I underline, "_Sympathy has its limits . . ._ "

"James?" I hear Ali call through the silence and the lack of light. I stand and put the book back in its spot. I know she knows, but I still don't want her to see me.

Margot

The third-period bell rings. It's Friday and Margot is exhausted by the week. She had gotten used to sleeping in and taking naps over the break.

James stands next to her as she leans on her locker. She looks thinner and there is some acne surfacing on her cheeks. She blinks her eyes, sometimes resting them closed for a moment before opening them again.

Margot takes a deep breath and exhales. She swallows, trying to get rid of the taste in her mouth. She forgot to eat something that morning, but it didn't really matter. The pills make her nauseous, and sometimes it is better not to have anything in your stomach than to risk vomiting.

"Hey," says Douglas, walking up and standing next to her. James rolls his eyes.

"Hey," she says with a small smile.

"I hate to tell you this, but Burns is looking for you. I overheard her ask a group of girls in the other hallway if they had seen you."

"Shit," says Margot, closing her eyes. "I am totally not up for Burns right now."

Douglas narrows his own eyes. "You doing okay? You look like you might not feel too well."

"I feel really nauseous," she says, shaking her head. "Tired."

"Why don't you go home?"

"I'll be okay. Just the medication. It comes and goes."

He studies her for a moment. "You sure? Want me to walk you to the nurse or something?"

"No," she says. "I think I just need some fresh air. I might go sit outside for a little while. Be a few minutes late for class, but oh well."

"Yeah, definitely do it if you think it will make you feel better."

She nods and closes up her locker.

"I'll see you after this period. Hope you feel better," he says, holding up a hand to wave goodbye. She smiles. As Douglas turns to leave, James concentrates hard and shoves him from behind. He goes flying onto the ground, and a couple of pencils roll out of his backpack.

He looks up at Margot in shock.

"Are you okay?" she asks. "Did you trip on something?"

"I'm fine," he says and gets to his feet. "But I have no idea how that happened." He shakes his head a little and continues down the hall.

James follows Margot as she takes slow, deliberate steps down the hallway towards the side door. She opens it and stands on the landing. For a minute she thinks she will just sit there, but then she remembers that Burns is looking for her. She checks over her shoulder to make sure that nobody is coming, and then she inches down the steps one by one and starts to walk over to Ali's tree.

"What's up with her?" Ali wonders, wide-eyed as Margot exhales loudly and sits down. There is a slight breeze, and she tilts her head backwards to welcome it.

"She's not feeling well," James answers in a monotone voice.

"What do you think is wrong with her?"

"I have no idea."

Ali looks at the girl, her head leaned back against the trunk of the tree, eyes closed, legs straight out in front of her. She looks paler than usual.

"She looks really thin," says Ali. "Was she always this thin?"

James shakes his head.

He sits down next to her and strokes her hair a couple of times. She raises a hand to her head and does a lazy scratch.

"Aw, James," Ali says, studying the sadness on his face.

"She'll be okay. Maybe just leave her alone for a bit. She could probably use some sleep."

"It's the middle of the day, Ali," James says.

"I know. I know what you're saying."

"I wish I could help her."

Ali nods. "Let's hope you can."

James

I decide that I should back off. If I am going to upset the balance of things, I'm not going to upset Margot also. I want to tell her how worried I am. How awful she looks. But I can't if I also want to keep her. And never mind the question of whether that is the right thing to do or not.

As I sit in the library I picture the old her for a while. I remember her sitting on the floor of my room talking at the old me, my dog Bear going back and forth between us, unsure of where he wanted to settle. She would talk over me as I lay on my bed doing my homework, and occasionally I would just grunt acknowledgment with the highs and lows of her voice, her bracelets jangling when she talked with her hands. I close my eyes and try to imagine the sound of all of it.

I had gotten pretty good at doing both things—listening to Margot and doing my work. I could tell by her tone when I really needed to pay attention or when she was just recounting something meaningless that had happened during the day. And she never demanded my full attention. We both just knew that she liked to talk more than I did. I realize how much I miss knowing things.

I flip for a while in the evening stillness of the library, and then finally I underline, *"It is invariably saddening to look through new eyes at things."*

Margot

Margot is late for school. She almost didn't come at all but as hard as it is for her to make it through the day at St. Xavier, she can't stand being at home. James watches as she walks up the steps. She never picks up her head. She sighs before she walks in the entrance.

He follows her.

Her steps are slow. They almost seem painful as she makes her way to the office to sign in. When she opens the door the room is buzzing. Telephones are ringing, the photocopier is droning, there are soft conversations everywhere.

She approaches the secretary's desk.

"Hi, I'm signing in," she croaks and then clears her throat.

"Name?"

"Margot Cramer."

The woman behind the desk looks up and then quickly looks back down and begins writing her name.

"Reason for tardiness?"

"Um, I wasn't feeling well."

The woman looks up again. "But you're feeling better now?"

Margot nods.

"You weren't feverish or anything?"

"No."

"Vomiting?"

"No."

"Well, what do you think was wrong then?" This time she looks up at Margot and focuses her gaze on her.

Margot starts to shift back and forth on her feet. She crosses her arms.

"I mean, I don't know. I might have just eaten something bad."

"Because you look like you still don't feel too well."

Margot closes her eyes and then opens them. "I'm fine . . . I wouldn't be here if I still felt sick. I would have just stayed home."

"Okay then. Grade?"

"Tenth."

"Do you have a parent's note?"

Margot slides her backpack off one shoulder, reaches around to grab a note out of it, and then hands it to the lady. "My mom said she was going to email, too."

"Okay, so what do you have second period?"

"Math."

"I'll give you a pass."

When she leaves the office, she takes small steps down the hallway. She pauses once, sipping from one of the water fountains. James notices that she splashes some of the water on her face.

She keeps going, takes two steps, and then reverses direction back to the water fountain. This time she looks both ways down the hallway and then opens a zipper pocket on her bag, removing a brown plastic pill bottle. She fumbles with the white top, grunting as she finally gets it removed.

With one finger she scoops out a pill and pops it into her mouth, leaning down again to get some water from the fountain. She wipes her mouth with the edge of her sleeve, slings her backpack back over her shoulder, and continues the slow walk to her class.

James couldn't make out the label on the bottle, and it's all he can do to resist the urge to run over and pull it out of her pack. He is beginning to feel angry at her, and he doesn't want to.

He sits in an empty desk in the back as Margot hands the late pass to the teacher without making eye contact. Sometimes in moments like this he wonders what he would say to her if he was alive, but he is certain this wouldn't be happening if he was. He feels the numbing trying to smooth out the rough edges of his feelings, and he puts his head down on the desk.

Margot takes out a pencil and opens her binder. She shifts on the hard desk chair, thinking for a moment how much more comfortable she'd be at home. Taking a deep breath she looks up at the board to start taking notes. When she lifts her hand to write she notices that it is shaking. She lifts the other one up beside it and holds it there until she realizes it is doing the same thing. She feels her heart pounding in her chest. Fifteen more minutes and then she can go to the library and calm down.

James

My eyes flutter open to an empty classroom. I lift my head and blink at the equations on the board as I try to focus my blurry eyes. Out of my peripheral vision I catch red swirling lights.

Anxiety surges through me. I remember those lights. The sound of sirens starts to reverberate throughout my head until I feel numb.

I force myself to stand, but I'm unstable. I hold my head and stagger toward the door. I manage to get into the hallway, but then I have to crouch down, holding my head again.

I try to shake some of the dizziness away. I stand and tilt my head from side to side, shake out my arms. A little better, but I still feel off.

What just happened? Why had I been in such a deep sleep that I didn't wake up when the bell rang or the class left?

I have no idea what time it is. School is still in session. There are students around and some of the classrooms have lights on and occupied desks. I decide to go to the library to see if Margot is there.

I pass the glass library windows. People are studying, and Ms. Perez is behind her desk. Maybe I haven't been asleep for too long.

I make my way toward the regular table looking for Margot, but there is no sign of her. The caged clock on the wall catches my eye. 1:45 pm. I had been asleep for a while!

I head for the F section. It is possible Margot has come and gone already.

The edge of the book is sticking out slightly on the shelf. I take it over to the windowsill and open it quickly. The pencil hits the ground as I read, *"Blessed are the dead that the rain falls on."*

"Hey!" I hear a voice say and look up. "Hey, James! I've been looking for you." Ali, with a distressed expression on her face, is rushing towards me. "Where've you been?"

"Here," I shrug. "Why?"

"This is my third trip here. And I didn't see you there when it happened, so I wanted to make sure that you knew."

"Knew what?"

"It's Margot."

"What about her?"

"They took her away . . . by ambulance," she says.

"What do you mean? Why?" I shove the book back onto the shelf.

"I can't say for sure. You know how they all talk, and I only got there for the end of it. One of them in the crowd was saying . . . overdose." She says the last word more quietly.

My mouth hangs open as I stare at her pinched face.

"But they were driving really slowly when they left. It didn't seem like a total emergency if that makes you feel any better."

"It doesn't," I say, standing, and I start to run.

"Gabriella was there. You should ask her. She might know more," she calls after me.

As I sail through the gym, I notice that there are two coaches chatting in the corner. One is mimicking basketball motions as he recounts gameplays to the other. I almost forget about them both as I go to bang open the double doors to the lounge outside for dramatic effect, but then catch myself.

"What happened?" I ask as I glide through the closed doors instead.

Stewart is tracing the cracks in the pavement with a stick. Gabriella had been stretched out looking at the sky but now turns her head in my direction.

"What happened?" I repeat when our eyes meet.

She sits up. "With what?"

"With Margot!"

She glances over at Stewart and then back at me. "I don't know. Why?"

"She was taken away by ambulance earlier today. I didn't know about it because I fell asleep in one of the classrooms this afternoon."

Stewart stares at Gabriella.

"I'm sorry," she says.

"Neither one of you saw anything? Heard the ambulance come?"

"Well . . . ," says Gabriella.

"Ali said she saw you there!"

Her eyes widen and she sighs. "I was going to tell you, James. Stewart and I were just discussing it."

"I didn't see it," says Stewart, holding his hands up in a surrender position.

"Like I said," says Gabriella, standing, "I was going to tell you, James. I was just worried because it seems like something bigger is going on than what happened to Margot today. I was concerned, and I wanted to talk to Stewart about that first."

"You know how worried I have been about her!"

"I know. I promise I was going to find you, and I was going to tell you all about—"

"It happened hours ago!" I yell.

"I understand. Please believe me. I was going to find you and let you know."

"Ali found me! Ali let me know!"

Gabriella sighs. She opens her mouth to say something but then just shakes her head.

"She had a reason for not finding you first, James," Stewart says. "She's worried there's a major fluctuation coming. The energy of the school is shifting. That might mean a lot more people than just Margot are vulnerable."

I shake my head and roll my eyes. "That doesn't even make any sense!"

"James," Gabriella starts, but I turn to go.

"Save it!" I yell on my way out. "I should have known you were both full of shit!"

Douglas

He didn't see it. Several of the girls were teary-eyed when Alicia Jones was telling him about it. "Her eyes were, like, rolling back in her head and stuff," she said, her distress evident on her face.

I can't even go ask if she's okay, he thinks. They're probably looking for him already.

He pictures her being hauled off on a gurney. Her pale face surrounded by her bright hair. Was she scared? Was she even awake? When he blinks he feels a tear rush down each cheek, and he rubs them away with the outside of his hands, takes a deep breath.

She didn't deserve it. She didn't deserve what was happening to her. So much of it was grief over something that wasn't her fault.

"Please be okay," he whispers into the air. "Please be okay." Maybe he should have left her alone. He probably made it worse somehow.

He slides his back down the wall and sits. They'll be looking for him soon if they aren't already. Just like with Ali.

He had stayed quiet through all the interrogations then. The screaming phone call from her hysterical mother. The phone call from Clinton, when he had just hissed, "Don't say anything" and then hung up.

No, he had not brought Ali home. He left the party before her.

Why?

He didn't say anything about the upstairs bathroom, where she had been all night. He didn't say anything about her flirting with Clinton for weeks.

So why did he leave before her?

He was tired.

Who was she with then?

He didn't know.

The others all said she didn't stay. They didn't know what

happened to her, where she went before she found her way into her bedroom at home, where she'd curl up to sleep and never wake up. That image still kept him up at night.

There was another one of the notes this morning. He wished he could report them but nobody would believe him and he needs to lay low.

"Again?" this one said, all in cut out black letters.

He has a lawyer now. They're reinvestigating everything, asking about text messages from that night.

His body shakes with silent sobs as he buries his head in his arms. This time there was no bathroom upstairs. No Clinton. This was on his watch. Whatever happened to Margot, he should have helped her. He missed something, and it was his fault. Or maybe he even made it happen.

"I'm sorry," he whispers. "I'm so sorry."

James

I sit on the steps the same way I do every morning, and I think about how it's amazing that they just carry on as if everything is normal. Was I also this oblivious to people suffering around me? They keep coming up the steps, laughing, pushing back and forth, shouting before they get into the building. How many times was I that clueless person? And which of them would care for Margot if I didn't?

I know I will not see her face in this crowd, but I'm hoping to see Douglas and follow him. See if I can get any other information. But as the last of the stragglers enter the building, I realize that's not going to happen, so I swing my legs over the side of the wall and wander inside.

I walk towards the main office thinking maybe I will hear something there. Pausing by the door, I remember when I arrived here like this, when I thought I was still alive, and punched the window to get in, dialed 911. The window had been repaired the next day. Everything had been chalked up to a student prank. Like I'd never been there looking for help.

I haven't been in the office for some time, but some things never change. There is the same cardigan draped over the back of Sister Ellen's chair, the same constant ringing of phones, the same conversations that carry on in loud whispers from the corners as guidance counselors talk with students and mix with the secretary shouting messages to people.

I make my way over to Mrs. Burns' office. I can hear her voice, low and muffled by the door. I hesitate and then decide to go in.

She is leaning back in her chair, her chubby legs crossed, flexing and unflexing her feet.

"I understand," she says. She scribbles something on a yellow legal pad next to her. "I may not have time to meet with him until tomorrow afternoon. Would that be okay?"

She listens for another moment or two, and I think I see her roll her eyes.

"Okay then. Yes, I will see if I can get him in here tomorrow afternoon and we will talk about this . . . Yes. You're welcome."

She puts the phone back on the receiver and breathes a heavy sigh. I scan the room, looking for any sign of a Margot update anywhere. There are many sticky notes on her desk, but none of the messages or notes have Margot's name on them anywhere. Books lining the small brown shelves have titles such as *Navigating the Teenage Mind* and *What to Expect When You're Expecting a Teenager.* I picture Margot staring at them during her sessions.

Mrs. Burns clears her throat and then says, "Oh!" out loud, snapping her fingers. She propels herself out of the chair with both arms, opens her door, and continues out into the hallway.

"Jeanine! You know what I meant to tell you?" she calls.

The screen of her computer glows blue and flickers. I look closer. Her email inbox is displayed. I scan the subject lines as Mrs. Burns' voice continues to chat away outside.

There are emails from teachers with subject lines like "Avery Third Period Chemistry." At this point, I've heard many conversations about students from teachers sitting in the teachers' lounge, but I'm curious to see what their emails look like.

I click the mouse. "Avery Johnstone's grades in chemistry continue to go downhill and behavior has become an issue as well. Can we please meet with him before parents to see if there is anything we need to be aware of?"

I go back to the inbox and scan. Nothing that looks like it might contain the information I'm looking for. I stand up straight instead of hunching over the computer screen and think for a minute. Then I lean back over and switch to the "sent" box.

There it is. Five down from the top. "Cramer" sent to Principal Logan.

"I spoke with Mrs. Cramer this morning. Margot remains in serious condition. They are concerned about possible organ damage and monitoring her very closely. She also expressed concern about Douglas Arsenault. She feels that perhaps something was given to Margot by him. Perhaps we should consider a locker check? Would you prefer meeting with him alone prior to a parent meeting? I am not completely convinced that this wasn't self-induced. Thanks, Delores Burns."

"Okay then!" I hear Mrs. Burns call. She is laughing and the sound is coming closer. I fumble to get the email closed and flip back to the inbox as she enters back into the office, but my fumbling back and forth causes the screen to flicker and catches her eye.

"This darn thing acting up again?" she says to herself, pulling out her desk chair and sitting down. I jump back to get out of her way.

"Alright . . . ," She stretches and exhales before she begins to click on emails.

"Let's have him meet with me first," she types to Avery's chemistry teacher, "and we'll see if I can get to the bottom of anything. I'll set something up with him."

I turn to leave. I think of Margot in a hospital bed and wonder if she's awake. Self-induced? Meaning she planned to harm herself? I think of the quote she left for me that day. *Blessed are the dead that the rain falls on.* Did she write that because she had this planned?

I pause by the door, hating the disconnect between us now. At least when she was here, there was the book. The book.

I move on before any more feelings of guilt can set in and check the hallway for Gabriella or Stewart before I dash outside.

"I need to ask you a question," I say, running to where Ali sits underneath the tree. She is drawing in the dirt with a small stick. "Do you think it's my fault?"

She looks up at me with a blank expression. "Do I think what is your fault?"

"What happened to her."

"Oh, with Margot? Is that what you mean?" She goes back to doodling.

"Yes, Margot. What happened to her."

She considers it a moment before answering. "No. I don't think it's your fault."

"I read one of Burns' emails. She kind of hinted that Margot might have done it to herself."

"Well, you obviously know her a lot better than I do. What do you think?"

"I don't know! I don't think it's something she'd do, but I just feel like maybe I messed with her sanity or something." Ali just stares back at me.

"I don't know the answer to that," she finally says. "In some ways, it was probably comforting, but at the same time, it was probably confusing. I don't think being confused necessarily makes you want to harm yourself though."

"Yeah, but maybe being confused and depressed does?"

"I'm going to be honest with you, James, and maybe you won't like it, but sometimes out of morbid curiosity, I tend to watch Douglas." She pauses and draws a sharp line in the dirt. "It fascinates me how he can go about his business here like nothing's different. Like he never left me with those idiots. Like I didn't *die* because of it! Anyway," she says, regaining her composure, "sometimes she looked pretty happy."

"She wasn't happy," I mumble.

"Okay. Well, how do you know that then?"

"I just do."

"So maybe it's no more than this, James. Maybe what happened to you shouldn't have happened and because it did, then this, whatever it is that is happening to her, shouldn't happen either."

"Can I ask you something else?"

"Why stop now?" she smirks.

"Did you remember me?"

She raises her shoulders into a small shrug.

"What do you mean?"

"When you first saw me? Did you know who I was?" I stare at her, waiting for her to answer.

"I recognized you. I mean, we weren't really friends, James. But why are you asking me this?"

"Something they said one time. About what you remember and you don't."

"What did they say?"

"Something about how you die sometimes has an effect on it. Sometimes I feel like they are surprised that I remember so much."

Ali nods. "But maybe they're not. Maybe they get it completely, but they don't want you to be attached for some other reason."

"I'm just so confused," I say, sitting down and shaking my head. "How did you . . . I mean, how did you even get into that stuff anyway?" I quickly study her face to see if I've offended her, but she is staring off into the street, expressionless.

"I don't know. It sort of just happened. A progression, I guess."

"Really?"

"Well, I mean, some of those guys that Douglas hangs out with, they're kind of . . . limit pushers, I guess. In some ways I guess that was really exciting to me at the time. My dad moved to Texas with his girlfriend, my mom was melting down, nothing I'd been doing right all my life really felt that good anymore. I know it sounds a little deep, but I've had a lot of time to think about things." She smiles.

"I can understand that a little."

"I guess I was angry too. Acting out. All that kind of stuff." We are quiet for a couple of minutes and then she continues, "But see, that's what I don't get. It's what I've never been able to make sense of here from day one. I act like a stupid teenager and I make some dumb mistakes and it costs me my life?"

"Some people might argue that heroin is a pretty big mistake," I say softly.

She exhales. "I don't know how it got to that. Or why it didn't seem like a big deal at the time, but it just didn't. I guess I was just swept up in feelings for Douglas, and hanging out at Delaney's house all the time opened up this whole new social life that I'd never had and, well, just this whole sense of liberation. I know it sounds like a cliché, but it just felt like nothing could happen to us. Like we invented being teenagers or something. And I just stopped being scared. Scared to get a bad grade or to skip practicing my cello or of what my parents would say or do." She pauses and shrugs. "Anyway, we tried it once or twice, little bits here or there, and I'm not going to lie, it was really fantastic. I wanted it that night. It was me who asked for it."

"Well, don't be mad at me for asking this," I begin, "but if you wanted it, why do you blame Douglas?"

"I don't blame him for me wanting it. I guess I had become a little attached and he was pulling away. It started to feel like it had all been a game to him. You know, get the little nerd girl to start hanging with your crowd and doing things she would have never done. But then I was in it, and I didn't want to leave it. I didn't want to let go of those feelings. I didn't want to go back to being scared again. But then he abandoned me at the party with Clinton, and I remember just feeling really humiliated. Like everyone knew he didn't really like me. So I just spent the evening completely high with Clinton. Somehow they managed to get me inside my house quietly, lay me down on the couch. That's where they found me the next morning. He didn't even tell my mother the truth about what I had done when they were trying to save me."

It was getting late. Traffic was starting to pick up and I was shocked that Ali was talking so much. I was trying to digest her words.

"I get it," I say. "But it did happen that way. You don't feel like there's maybe a natural order to things or something that we are not supposed to mess with?"

"I already told you how I feel about that," she says, her wistful tone changing. "I don't think fate always gets it right. And now I know we can go back and try again."

I nod.

"And," she says standing up, "I know how to do it."

"You do?" I ask, staring up at her. She nods. "How?"

She stares back at me for a moment and then says, "I don't want them to know," with a serious look on her face.

"I'm not going to tell them, Ali. I'm going with you."

"But what if you change your mind?"

"I'm not going to. And does it matter really? I mean, they're going to know you're gone once you've left."

"I know that. But they could just think that I've moved on to the next level. Maybe I heroically performed the life-changing events that I needed to," she says, taking a little bow.

"I'm pretty sure they'll figure it out."

"I'm not sure of much here," she says, "but I do know that I'm leaving soon. And I don't care where they think I went."

Without the library and the book to occupy me I have much more time on my hands than usual to kill.

I decide to go outside and sit on the bleachers, the same exact spot that I spent my first night as a ghost. I know I won't sleep, but at least I might be able to reflect for a while on what Ali said.

I manage to avoid the others most of the evening. At one point I had rounded a bend and saw Stewart at the end of the hallway. I lifted my hand to wave and Stewart had done the same, but I kept going, trying to make it obvious that I didn't want to talk. He didn't come after me, so I guess he got it.

I miss the way the bleachers used to squeak when I walked up them, how they announced your presence.

What would I say to Margot right now? It had become like a puzzle trying to get the book to speak for me. Maybe I should have just flat out left her a note. Why had I never done that?

It's something I have thought about a lot, and I think it was because the shred of doubt was safer. I wanted her to know it was me, but never really be one hundred percent sure, just in case that was too much to digest. If she comes back, will she look for the book again? Will she even come back?

"Please don't run away," I hear Gabriella's voice say. "I just want to say hello."

"Hello. I'm not going to run away, but I am out here because I want to be alone."

"I get that. I won't stay. I guess I just felt like I need to apologize again."

I am silent.

"I stand by the fact that I was trying to help a situation. But I should have found you. I should have let you know." She rocks herself back and forth.

"I agree," I finally say.

"I'm sorry I wasn't a better friend. I feel like I really messed up our relationship and I regret that very much."

"It's alright, Gabriella," I reply in an even-toned voice, staring at the track in front of me. "We never really had a relationship anyway, did we? I died, I ended up here, you told me what you thought I needed to know in order to get by."

"Well, I mean . . ."

"We weren't really friends at all, were we?"

"I'd like to think—"

"No," I interrupt. "Friendships are give and take. I was just taking." She looks off to the side. "I didn't see it that way."

"No, I was. I was just needy, and you constantly gave me information." She shifts her weight and purses her lips.

"And now I just don't really know about your *information*, Gabriella."

"I never lied to you. Everything that I ever told you was true. It was just this one time, with Margot, because I thought you needed—"

"Look, this *situation*, this whatever it is, is confusing enough. I don't need to spend any more time trying to figure out if you're lying to me because of what you think I need, or maybe even more so because of what you need."

"I know Ali is probably telling you things, things that you really want to believe," says Gabriella, lowering her voice. "But you shouldn't."

"Shouldn't you send Stewart to deliver that message? Because it doesn't work so well coming from you."

"I understand you're angry," she begins and takes a deep breath. "But there's more to it than you realize. I promise you that."

"I'm not in the mood for this, Gabriella. You've said hello, you've said you're sorry. What you don't seem to understand is that I am worried sick about someone who doesn't deserve what is happening to her."

"And what would you have done for her in that particular situation? If you knew?" Her usually emotionless voice contains a little bit of hurt. "Would you have jumped in and tried to save her? Lifted her off the ground? Held her hand? Whispered words of encouragement to her? None of that was possible, James!"

I blink, trying to erase the image of Margot like that from my mind.

"I'm sorry but it wasn't," she continues.

"It's not up to you to decide that!"

"You're right, it's not! And really, it's not up to you either! It's just the way it is."

"Just save it, okay? I don't really need to hear any more about the way things are from you."

She sighs, and we are silent.

"Anyway, I apologize. I should have found you and let you know what I had seen."

I nod.

"Just be careful, okay? I know you don't want to believe me, but if I'm right about what I think is happening, and Ali is hearing things about leaving here, it's dangerous. And wrong."

"Why was nobody watching Margot?" I ask her. She opens her mouth to speak but I interrupt her. "Why are we worrying about other stupid stuff when she was in trouble?"

"I know it's not what you want to hear, but because we weren't told to. She wasn't a mission for us, James."

I laugh. "Goodbye," I say, finally turning to look at her.

She nods, lingers a moment, and then turns to leave.

I stand outside Mrs. Burns' office, waiting for her to be called out for some reason so that I can access her email again. Yesterday I tried to watch which keys she hit as she typed in her password but couldn't make it out. She's a fast typer.

"Delores?" One of the secretaries makes her way across the office and knocks on the door. I stand in anticipation but then sit again as they continue to have a conversation in the doorway.

I can see Steven Galloway make his way to the principal's office, and I smile. Some things never change. And then, on the other side of the office, I see Douglas stroll in and go to the sign-in sheet.

I clench my jaw and stare. He's got a weird combination of confident swagger and little boy nervousness. He runs his hands through his shaggy hair a lot. Did he give Margot something? Had he hurt her? He couldn't have possibly, as Ali suggested, made her happy.

Residuals bump around the office with their usual facial expressions of normalcy, as if of course they are supposed to be there.

"Hey." Stewart appears next to me, having come through the wall that closes off the main hallway.

"Hey," I say, looking up at him from the chair.

"What are you doing?"

"Snooping."

Stewart smiles. "Fair enough." He folds his arms and looks around Burns' office.

"Look, Stewart, I know what you guys think and you can tell Gabriella I'm over it, but—"

Stewart holds up his hand. "Not why I am here."

"Alright, that's fine, I just really don't want to hear any more about who's right and who's wrong and all that kind of stuff."

Stewart shrugs. "Well, I wasn't here to talk about that kind of stuff, but okay. I just wanted to see if you wanted to go for a run. Haven't seen you in a few days, thought it might be fun."

"Thanks, man. I'm good." I smile.

"Well, we do miss you. Gabriella feels really bad. And if you are getting information about how you can be anywhere else but here, we should talk about that."

"How is that even possible? We have to be here, right? We're protectors." I meet his eyes. He just blinks at me. "It's fine. Really. I just need some space."

Stewart nods. "Okay." He pauses for a moment and then disappears back through the wall.

I feel an emotion that I can't pinpoint. I'm not exactly sad, but something about Stewart's departure, the sight of his back zooming through the wall, bothers me.

I look over towards the sign-in sheet again. One of the secretaries has come around from behind the desk and is talking to Douglas. They start to walk towards Mrs. Burns' office together.

"Principal Logan made it very clear to your father that you were supposed to check in with Mrs. Burns first thing in the morning. I believe there's a meeting with all of you together after school."

"Yeah, I knew about that one," Douglas replies, nonplussed.

I shift out of the way and frown as Douglas moves to sit down in the same seat I was sitting in. I give him the middle finger as his watery eyes stare in my general direction. The secretary knocks on Mrs. Burns' door.

"Delores?"

"Come in!"

"The Arsenault child to see you."

"Oh yes, alright, send him on in."

Douglas stands up with an annoyed look on his face, sighs, and turns to open her door.

"Mr. Arsenault! Good to see you," I hear her say.

Douglas closes the door, but I go right through it. I stand, arms folded, in the corner of Mrs. Burns' office, observing the conversation.

"I really don't know why I have to be here," Douglas says, slumping into her ugly couch.

"How's your friend?"

"Which one?" he asks.

"I'm speaking about Margot Cramer."

"I don't really know. Her mom is not letting her have her phone or something."

"That's not the case, Douglas. I don't believe she's able to use her phone. I can let you know, though, that her condition is serious."

Douglas blinks. "Yeah, I . . . I mean, I kind of figured it was since she isn't back yet."

"Do you know what happened to her?"

He shakes his head.

"Don't know what could have caused her to collapse at school?"

Douglas shakes his head again. "I mean, I think she'd been pretty tired. Maybe she was sick or something too? I'm sure other people could tell you. She has other friends, you know."

Mrs. Burns smiles, sits back in her chair, and crosses her legs.

"She did. But not many. And I'm told she'd become particularly close to you."

He shrugs. "I don't really know."

"Well, I do," she says. "And I am not going to violate her confidentiality, but we are seriously concerned about her well-being. And perhaps we need to be concerned for yours as well."

Douglas widens his eyes and glances around the room. "Why?"

"Well, that's what I was hoping you might discuss with me in advance of the meeting with your parents and the principal later. I thought it might be easier to discuss any problems you found yourself having before we are all together."

"I don't have any problems," he says, his face expressionless. "If she does, it does not mean I do. I mean, I really just got to know her recently, and obviously, she's been through a lot this year."

Mrs. Burns nods. "It's true. She has. And everyone is very aware of that."

"So?" he says, shaking his head and shrugging.

"I wanted to take the opportunity, Douglas, to see if there was anything you needed to talk about with me."

"No," he says, stretching his arms and resting them behind his head, "there is not."

"Okay then. We can just meet later with your parents."

"I don't really get why we have to, but okay."

"Just concerned about you, that's all."

He scoffs.

She reaches over and takes a sip of water from a paper cup on her desk. She reaches to put the cup back down on the desk without looking and misjudges it—spilling water on her desk calendar. I look down as she blots at it with tissues and notice that she has "locker check" written and circled on today.

"James!" Ali comes flying through Burns' closed office door and stops in her tracks at the sight of the meeting. "Sorry. I thought you were in here searching emails."

"Nope!" I say, smiling and motioning to the conversation still going on in front of us. Burns was saying something about being concerned for *all* the students in this school, regardless of any past mistakes.

Ali winces at the sight of Douglas, but then her expression changes back to the same excited one that she came in with.

"I know," Ali says, beaming at me. "I got the location."

"It's my fault." Gabriella's knees are drawn up to her chest and her arms are wrapped around them. Her voice is muffled because her head is bowed.

"You did what you thought was right," Stewart says, but she can detect the doubt hiding behind the reassurance.

"Stewart?"

"Yep?" He swats at the mosquitos that always swarm in the courtyard at this hour, enjoying their confusion from the gusts of air he creates.

"Maybe it wasn't so much that I was protecting him."

"What do you mean?"

She lifts her head up. "I was frustrated. I mean, it's hard to empathize with his attachment after being here so long. There were times when I wanted him to just stop it all and pay attention to what we're here to do."

"I had moments where I felt that way too," Stewart says.

"But that wasn't fair," she continues. "And now he's listening to Ali, and he doesn't even realize . . ." her voice trails off.

"I saw him today," Stewart says. "I tried to engage him, asked him if he wanted to go for a run."

"You did? What happened?"

"He didn't want to. He said he just needed some time to himself right now."

"That's the thing though, Stewart. He's not by himself. He's with her, getting all the information that we have been trying to protect them from."

"Look, I'm not happy about it either. But really, there is only so much that we can do. We know that. And it may be that we have to fight this a different way."

"I know that! But Stewart, if she's telling him he can go back, that would mean there would be a complementary variable and two—"

"I know. I know." Stewart lifts his hand up in the air and closes his eyes. "But he doesn't trust us right now. Anything we say to him is just going to feel like BS. I mean, come on, you know what it's like. Remember what it felt like when you found out that you can, I don't know, make it all go away."

She nods. "I just wish we could find a way to make him trust us again. So that we could undo all the damage."

"He doesn't see it that way though. He thinks he has found the truth. He thinks the truth is a matter of opinion."

"I knew Ali heard the whispers. It's why she would never check her graffiti." She exhales.

"We don't know how much she hears. Or what they have told her."

"We know from the residuals what she is planning. They wouldn't be freaking out if there wasn't going to be a major balance shift. If it wasn't shifting already."

"Nothing is done yet. But we can't overwhelm him. I think we need to give him his space."

"I just don't know how much time we have." Her tone is defeated and she stretches her legs out in front of her.

"I know," sighs Stewart. "I'm worried about that too."

"Guess where it is?" Ali says. She made me come out of Burns' office and out to the tree. "Your favorite place."

I shrug. "I didn't know I had one."

"The library!" she announces, beaming. She seems lighter and more kid-like than she ever has.

"Really?"

"Really, James. The whole time that you were sitting there conferring with the other world, your ability to go back to it was right underneath your nose."

"So how?" I briefly picture myself trying to jump inside a book or something.

"Okay, well, you know those really old pictures of the saints all over the walls in there?"

"Yup."

"One of them."

"Which one?"

"Ugh," she says, glancing up at the window, "she's there again. I'm just going to start waving." I glance up and catch what looks like a shadow breeze by the window. "See, this is why we came outside."

"What painting?"

"Oh! Well, that I don't know yet." She folds her arms and smiles.

"When do we get to go?"

"I don't quite know that either."

"So, we just know we go through one of the paintings of one of the saints at some point in time?"

"Yes," she says.

"Okay." I look out towards the street. Two cars honk at each other.

"You don't seem very excited."

"No, I am. I mean, I'm just anxious to go already. I'm sick of them lurking around me trying to tell me what to do." I gesture up towards the window. "And Margot is still in serious condition apparently. It all just sucks. I just . . . I just want to be there again."

"Look, I totally know what you mean. Once you know you can, and once you make the decision to, it's so hard to wait it out here. I've been waiting for a while, James, believe me." Her eyes look serious again.

"I just hope nothing happens to her," I say. "I just hope I get the chance to meet her again."

"Very romantic, Therioult," she says, rolling her eyes.

"It's not a romantic thing," I say, my voice sounding angrier than I mean for it to.

"Of course it's not."

"Whatever, it's not like that."

"Well, look at it this way: if she dies, maybe she'll end up here too and you can just stay."

"That's not funny. Besides, I am not just going back for her." I shrug and look all around me. "I just want out of here. I want to see the world again."

"Hear you on that one," she says.

"And she doesn't deserve to die."

"Neither did you," she snaps back, raising her eyebrows.

"Think it will be soon?" I ask.

"It has to be. I've never heard them as loudly as I do now."

"They're going to search her locker," I say to Ali. "And I am not sure if I should intervene."

"Why would you?" she asks, picking apart a leaf.

"Because if she's got something in her locker that could get her in trouble then maybe I should get it out."

"Well, why wouldn't you then?"

"Because if she's taking something she shouldn't be then maybe they need to know that to help her."

"I think they already know, James," she says, looking over at me and blinking. "I'm sure they tested her for different substances at the hospital."

"True," I say.

"But having them in your locker at school gets you in trouble on another level. So maybe you should help her out that way."

"I think I am going to," I say. "That's kind of what my gut is telling me to do."

Opening Margot's locker hurts. There are little familiar pieces of her everywhere—a brush with strands of her hair stuck in it, her white St. Xavier sweater with her initials written on the tag in her neat handwriting, "MC!" The numbing prods at me as I push a binder and a half-eaten granola bar to the side.

I wonder if I should be opening notebooks and textbooks and looking for things. I see an envelope wedged in the back so I pull on it. It's thin and crumpled and looks like it's been there for a little while. It's addressed to Margot and has a return address of "Everton Fine Arts, New York, NY." I pull the thin letter out of the envelope and read:

> Dear Ms. Cramer,
>
> We are delighted to offer you admission to Everton Fine Arts School for your junior and senior years of high school. We were impressed with your application and supporting materials and think you will make a fine addition to the program. Please return the enclosed contract by the stated deadline with your deposit. We are looking forward to having you on campus!
>
> Sincerely,
> Adelaide Wescott
> Dean of Admissions

I read it twice before the reality of it sinks in. She applied to school in New York. She was leaving. And she never told me.

I stuff the envelope back in and slam the locker door. I stand and stare at it in disbelief, unable to talk myself into moving until I can come up with some answers. Why would she not tell me? Why did she even apply in the first place?

"Hey," Ali says, turning the corner into the hallway. "Find anything?"

"Nope," I say, staring at the locker door a moment before turning to face her. "Nothing important."

The next day, Ali still has no news. She'll barely leave the tree, convinced that she may hear a whisper in the breeze that will give us the answers that we need. But the days are long and the branches aren't moving.

Sometimes I sit with her longer than I want to, hoping that maybe there's a way I might hear something that she doesn't. But mostly it's because I don't know what else to do with myself. I wonder if Stewart and Gabriella are trading notes on students in the faculty lounge and then following them around like paparazzi. "It's how we know how to help them," I hear Gabriella's voice say in my head. I roll my eyes.

I'm still reeling from the letter in Margot's locker. I can't believe she never talked to me about it and that I will never know why. I picture the giant embossed "E" at the top of the thick cream-colored paper.

But it's an easier decision now that I know she is leaving for school in New York. I can go back and not have to do everything in my power to make sure she doesn't become a protector too. I shake my head to clear the thoughts.

"I don't get it," I say to Ali as she leans against the trunk of the tree, eyes closed. "Where are they? Why did they only give us half of the directions?"

She shrugs without opening her eyes. "They come and go, James. I really don't know why."

The final bell rings and the students pour out of the doors like they are escaping a fire. Yesterday I read an email to the principal on Burns' computer that Margot had been released from the hospital. "No return date planned just yet," Burns had said. The principal's reply was, "Team meeting needed with parents and coordination plan for counseling/ further support if she is to return."

But relief had flooded over me at the first line: "MC released from hospital. Recovered and resting comfortably at home."

I stand and say, "I think I might go to the library for a while. Do some reading."

The book isn't where it should be, but that is my own doing. I've hidden it at the end of the aisle now for safekeeping. Every once in a while I'll pull it from its misfiled spot on the shelf and read our underlined passages as quickly as I can, pretending it's a conversation.

I sit still for a moment, second-guessing myself for the thousandth time on whether or not I contributed to what happened to Margot. And then I find what I would want to tell her.

"So I walked away and left him standing there in the moonlight— watching over nothing."

I mark the page with the pencil and close the book.

The locker room is empty. I push up the metal clasp to open the doors and sit down on the bench in front of my locker. They have never remembered to clean it out. I stare at my shoes, examine the frayed edge of the lace on the right one that had been driving me crazy. I touch the stiff tank top that I still use to run with Stewart sometimes. Staring at the contents it seems to me for the first time like a memorial to someone who no longer exists instead of a collection of my everyday items. I think about that for a moment. "No longer exists." And yet, here I sit.

I cringe as the door to the locker room is thrown open and the space explodes with the voices of the basketball team. Some are laughing, taunting, or yelling just to yell. The way they echo off the walls in the small concrete place is a familiar sound that I don't miss. Someone slams my locker shut to reach the one next to it. I close my eyes and listen to the activity around me.

"James?" a voice shouts above the rest.

When I open my eyes I see Gabriella in the corner, looking from side to side. There is a residual stretching on the bench in front of me, partially blocking her view.

"James?" she calls. "I'm pretty sure you're still here." A boy throws a sweaty towel at someone right in front of her, and she cringes. "This is my last attempt to talk to you, I promise," she calls out. "And you know I'm serious about it if I am in here right now."

I sway to keep up with the residual's stretching motion and stay hidden.

"James, I think you and Ali might have some bad information. You are supposed to be here and there are some really terrible things that can happen if you find a way out. Please let me explain them to you. People could get hurt . . ." she pauses, waiting for a response, and then adds, "badly."

I consider yelling back to her to leave me alone. But I'm not in the mood for her to challenge me or plead with me to listen anymore. I just want to think about going back and starting fresh. I don't want to spoil that by listening to her talk about the order of things.

"James?" She calls out again as some boys start to exit the locker room. "I'm seriously begging you at this point."

When her head is turned in the other direction I zip into a bathroom stall, sit on the toilet, and pull my feet up so that I'm not visible to her. I look at the graffiti on the metal walls.

"Blake sucks."

"Frank crapped here," with a running stick count underneath it.

"Coach Mullins is an aZZhole."

"Gertrude."

I laugh silently at the first few.

"Alright, fine. I'm leaving," Gabriella's voice quivers a little. I hear the faint sound of a rush of wind, and I look back again at the graffiti, waiting to make sure she is really gone before I leave the stall.

"Gertrude," catches my eye again. The writing pulsates and changes to glittery green. I sit and watch it, waiting for it to stop, but it doesn't.

As we sit underneath the tree and Ali sleeps, I am having second thoughts. I can't tell her this of course, but as I stare out at the nothingness of the night, I don't know what I'm going back for anymore. Margot was leaving me, and she hadn't even told me. Worse yet, she never even told me she was thinking about it. And if she ever comes back to St. Xavier after this, will she just gravitate right back to Douglas or will the new me even have a shot?

I picture her back home now, resting upstairs under her favorite quilt. I throw a pebble out into the blackness.

The Margot who was my best friend before she was my girlfried, the one who I climbed trees and rode bikes with, and the Margot who was my girlfriend—who I can still remember exactly what it feels like to hold in my arms—neither of those Margots is who I thought they were. And maybe we were not what I thought we were.

At least I wouldn't be stuck inside this school twenty-four hours a day anymore, but maybe moving on to the next place from here, maybe whatever comes next once I've stayed and helped the people I am supposed to help, is even better than going back. I look over at Ali and wonder if she's ever considered that. She shifts slightly but her eyes don't open.

Could I stay? And if I do, can I make it however much longer I'm supposed to be here? I am about to go for a run and mull it all over some more when she sits up.

"Hey," I say.

"Hey," she replies, rubbing her eyes.

"Hear something?"

"No," she shakes her head. "Sorry." She stretches and leans her back up against the trunk of the tree.

"Do you still trust them?" I ask as she starts to peel the bark off a stick.

"Yes. Definitely."

"Aren't you getting tired of just sitting here though?" I ask. "I mean, when they're ready to tell you, they'll tell you."

"What else am I going to do?"

"I don't know. I just feel like we should do something besides sit here."

"Well, you go right ahead!"

"I'm saying you too. *We* should go do something."

"Suggestions?"

"I don't know. Mark our departure from this somehow?"

She thinks for a moment and then smiles. "That might be fun. We'd have to figure out some good stuff though."

"I was thinking like a prank or something."

Her eyes light up.

"Nothing terrible."

"Alright, let's brainstorm then!"

"Something that doesn't break stuff or hurt anyone. I just want to make people, I don't know, wonder, I guess."

"Well, let's figure it out then."

It is two o'clock in the morning. The dim security lights of the library, the dull buzz of the caged clock, and the thump of moving books are the backdrop to our work.

"It's going to take a while," I say, turning another stack of books upside down.

"I know, but even if we only get halfway through it, it will be awesome!" Ali replies, finishing a shelf and stepping back to admire her efforts.

"Can you picture Ms. Perez's face when she opens the library in the morning?"

Ali laughs.

"What are you going to do about your, you know, special book?"

I shrug. "I don't know. I had been hiding it. I'll probably just put it back where it belongs. It will be the last thing they think of when they are trying to put them right side up."

"Think she'll look for it if she ever comes back?"

"I don't know. I kind of hope she does." I slide down and begin to turn books over on a new shelf. "Just let me know if you get to the Fs before I do."

"Will do." She laughs again. "Sorry, I just keep picturing the looks on their faces when they come in here in the morning."

"It's going to be good!" I agree.

"Hey, do you think Stewart and Gabriella will come in here tonight?"

"Hard to say. Stewart likes to be outside at night for the most part."

"Yeah, but Gabriella has been seriously stalking you."

"Tell me about it. I had to hide out from her the other day."

Ali shakes her head. "They're just pawns, James. They don't want you to know your options because then you won't be a pawn with them."

"Yep," I say, continuing to flip books.

"Looks fun," says a voice from the other side of the library. Stewart.

"Hey, Stewart," I say, trying not to sound startled.

"Hey. Good prank."

Ali pauses and looks over, expressionless.

"Yeah, thanks. We thought we'd just have a little fun."

Stewart nods and looks around. I try to gauge from his expression whether he is upset or not.

"We're not damaging anything," I finally say, breaking the silence. "We just wanted to have a little fun."

"No, I get it. It's good. Never thought of this one before." A small smile crosses his face, and I feel myself relax.

"Anyway, I was just passing by. Thought I'd say hello." He gives a small wave in Ali's direction, and she returns the gesture with a tight smile. "So hello!" he says, clapping his hands together.

"You're not usually inside at night," I say.

"Yeah, no, you're right. I was actually seeing if I could grab some of the voicemails off Nurse Kelly's phone. Mark Allen's appendix almost burst at school today. Seems like it was pretty serious."

"Keeping vigil in case you might need to bring someone new into the fray?" Ali says as she turns her attention back to flipping books. I freeze.

"Not really," says Stewart. "Seems like it's under control."

"Well, that's good," I jump in.

"It is."

Ali lets out a heavy sigh from her corner.

"Well, I'll leave you both to it then. Just wanted to say hi." He gives a mock salute and turns to leave.

"Yeah, thanks. Good to see you."

"You too," says Stewart, looking over his shoulder as he goes through the wall.

"Oh bullshit!" barks Ali the second he's gone. "He knows it's in here somewhere. He was just checking to see if we were going."

"You think?"

"Definitely."

"Well, another row completed!" I say, sliding down and brushing up against the wall. Half of my arm disappears into it without me willing it to. The picture above me catches my eye—a nun peering down with not a sad expression, but almost a calm curiosity. I look behind me at the gold plaque on the wall. "St. Gertrude," it reads.

"Ali . . . ," I say, my eyes fixated on it.

"Why didn't you tell me that?" her voice can't seem to decide between anger and excitement.

"I mean, I guess I didn't make the connection! It could have meant anything."

"And it changed colors, you said? The same way it did when you got Douglas's mission?"

"Yes. It changed colors."

She bites her bottom lip and then smiles. "This is it, James. They told us how to do it. They told *you!*" She takes a deep breath. "Now that it's here, I almost don't know what to do." She lifts her hand up to touch the picture.

"No!" I yell. "Don't make contact with it. I don't feel like we have all the instructions."

She pulls her hand back. "You're right. They always said they would make the time clear."

I nod and stare hard at the painting.

Ali looks up at the plaque and her eyes begin to mist. "Gertrude," she says and smiles. "I've been waiting a long time to meet you."

"What should we do now?" I ask.

"I think we should leave this and go back to the tree. Or maybe you should go back to the locker room. See if there is any other graffiti that doesn't quite make sense."

"Yeah, okay."

"Let's meet back under the tree in a while."

Gabriella resists the urge to call his name. Is it another trip down memory lane with the locker items, she wonders. He's been visiting them an awful lot lately. Besides, Stewart reported that they were busy with some prank in the library and not actually looking for a portal. She had been on the way to visit one of the class pets she loves, but she changes her route and goes through the wall to where she knows the locker room showers to be.

James is used to all the nighttime shadows in the gym, but he's also thinking about how this could be one of his last times looking at them. He takes in the shadows from the giant windows that stretch across the floor like figures in a funhouse mirror.

He feels like he should be extra careful with Stewart and Gabriella likely right outside the double doors at the end of the gym, but he's hoping for an uneventful trip to the locker room to check for any clues that he might have missed or even some new ones. If he does bump into one of them, his plan is to just say he was on the way to say hello. As much as the thought of idle chitchat right now pains him, it's just what he'll have to do. Especially with Gabriella. He does not realize that as he slips into the locker room, Gabriella emerges from outside just in time to see his back go through the door.

She pushes herself softly through the wall and into a shower stall. Then she listens. She definitely hears a locker open and then hears it close a minute or so later. Is he just retrieving something?

She waits and listens some more. Is that the sound of a bathroom stall? She wants to stick her head outside the shower stall to see but resists the urge.

It sounds like he clicked the lock of the stall. Suddenly she hears the spinning of a toilet paper roll. She shakes her head a little and smiles, perplexed. But seconds later she hears the door push open, and then there is no more noise at all.

She waits a while longer before going back out through the wall she had come in through. Even if he is in the gym, he might not see her emerge or he might assume she came through the doors that lead to the courtyard.

She steadies herself and goes through. Instead, she finds Stewart moving across the gym.

"Oh hey," he says, looking confused. "I was just coming to look for you."

"Didn't you say they were busy turning over all the books in the library?"

Stewart rolled his eyes slightly and nods. "Yeah, they were."

"Well, I just followed James in here. First to his locker and then to a bathroom stall."

Stewart squishes his face up in confusion.

"Wait here. See if he comes back," says Gabriella.

"I was just coming to find you!" Ali says as I return to the tree. She stands, though she looks exhausted.

"There was nothing new there," I say, shrugging.

"Well, there was here." She's beaming. "You were right about Gertrude. It's behind her painting. They've been getting our new lives in place, sending paperwork to the school and stuff. We're supposed to go in the morning. Check in at the office."

"Wow," I say, sitting down. "So starting tomorrow, no more this?" I say, lifting my arms up in the air and looking all around.

"No more this," Ali repeats. "Well, at least no more this *like* this."

I feel relief spread through me. I crouch down and hold my head in my hands.

"I know," Ali says. "I can hardly believe it either. FINALLY!" she yells up at the sky.

I wonder for a moment if Stewart and Gabriella are outside and can hear her screaming. But then, I realize that I don't care.

"So hours?" I say, looking up at her.

"Hours," she says and nods.

Gabriella waits. She hovers on the concrete stairs around the corner from the tree. Stewart thinks she's overreacting, but he didn't hear Ali scream like that. She sounded happy. Stewart said he thought they were just revved up from their prank, that if they knew how to cross they would already be gone.

She works up the courage to peer around the corner. They are still there, sitting as they have been for hours. Their eyes seem to be closed, and they're both sitting straight up against the trunk of the tree. It bothers her to see James sitting the same way Ali is. She sighs.

The sun is starting to come up. The peacefulness of the last hours of the night is about to be gone. There are more cars on the road.

Moments later she thinks she hears twigs snapping. She looks around the corner. They are standing. Ali's hands are on James' arms. She is telling him something. This is it. She thinks about going to get Stewart but there may not be time. If she's right they are going to the library. She's got to beat them there.

They are laughing when they enter. She hears them from the aisle that she is hiding in.

"Nope! Just as awesome as it was last night!" she hears Ali say. "Too bad we don't have time to finish it all."

"Yeah, maybe some other time," James says. His voice sounds nervous.

They are quiet for a moment.

"I mean, we know what to do. It just feels like we're supposed to close this out, or something . . . I don't know."

She begins to push the picture aside.

"Please don't do it," Gabriella says, stepping into the middle of the room.

Ali freezes, her hand on the portrait. James tilts his head back and looks at the ceiling. The library is silent until the air conditioning suddenly clicks on and makes a faint droning noise.

"Gabriella, just leave, okay? We don't want to help you anymore." Ali's voice is even but forceful.

Gabriella takes another step forward. "It's not about helping me. Or Stewart. I just can't believe you would choose to go when you know what will happen. *Do* you really know what will happen?"

"Yes," James says, folding his arms and staring at her.

"Then why?" Her voice cracks.

"Because we don't want this," Ali says, shaking her head and motioning all around her.

"None of us wanted this, Ali. We didn't end up here by choice." Gabriella takes another step. James' arms are still folded. He looks her up and down.

"We do have a choice, Gabriella," Ali says. "But if I didn't hear them, you never even would have told us."

"Because it's a false choice." She turns her head towards James. "What if they take Margot now?"

"They won't."

"You don't know that."

"She's not staying. She's going to a different school."

Gabriella looks at the floor. "It's not right. Whoever it is, it won't be their time."

"Maybe it wasn't ours!" Ali shouts.

"Please, just wait," Gabriella puts her hands in the air as if she is being held at gunpoint. "Let's all talk about it. I don't think you realize what you are going to start, everything that will happen if you do it."

Ali glares at her, then takes the portrait down off the wall and places it on the ground. A bright green circle pulsates and then fades.

"Please," Gabriella pleads. "Please don't!"

"Oh my goodness!" A voice sounds from the other side of the library. Lights begin to flick on. They turn to see Ms. Perez staring, mouth open, at the shelves of overturned books.

Gabriella turns her head back towards Ali, but she is gone. Her shoulders sink.

"What in the world?" they hear Ms. Perez exclaim as she walks around the library, taking everything in.

"Don't do it, James," Gabriella says, taking two slow steps closer and shaking her head. "You wouldn't do it if you knew."

"I'm not like you."

"Yes, you are!" Her eyes are welling up. Ms. Perez's footsteps are growing closer. "James, I'm begging you not to do it."

He glances over at one of the bookshelves in the distance and closes his eyes for a few seconds. Then he opens them and looks at her.

"Goodbye, Gabriella." When he is gone the pale green swirling circle fades back to the color of the wall.

Margot

Sister Ellen repositions her yellow sweater over the desk chair. The phone has just started to ring, but when she looks up she sees through the big glass window the one they have been waiting for coming down the hallway, so she hits the button on the phone, sending it to voicemail.

She puts her glasses on to see her better. She looks good. Not necessarily happy, but refreshed. Sister Ellen smiles as the girl opens the door.

"Hello!" she says as she approaches. The girl blinks, taken aback by her exaggerated cheerfulness.

"Hi," she replies quietly, tucking her hair behind her ear. "I need to check in. Margot Cramer."

"Yes, yes," she says, writing her name into the ledger on her desk before lowering her voice and saying, "I think it's been agreed upon that you'll meet with Mrs. Burns during first period?"

Margot smiles. "Yes, that's right," she says as the door opens and then slams behind her.

"Oops," says a tall girl that neither of them has seen before. "Sorry about that. I didn't realize the door was so heavy." She is hunched over, balancing a stuffed green backpack on one shoulder.

"That's alright, dear, but please do be more careful next time. Do you need to check in? Have you been out ill?"

"Oh no, we're supposed to stop here and drop off paperwork. New students," she says and smiles. "Just transferring in."

"Oh, well, welcome!" says Sister Ellen. "Just give me a

moment."

"Sure," she says and smiles at Margot. "Hi!"

"Hi," says Margot. "Welcome."

"Thanks," she says, still grinning and twisting her head all around to take in the room. "It's good to be here."

The door opens again and a boy walks in and stands behind her.

"My brother," the girl says. Margot smiles and nods.

"Hi," he says. "G-g-good to meet you."